THE OUTLAW SANDRA LOVE

A NOVEL BASED ON A TRUE STORY

Bennetti
Bestwing!
Steve Peters
Kay Roberts Stephens

KAY STEPHENS

STEVE PETERS

Published by Star Hill Publishing
345 Bahia Lane, Cape Carteret, North Carolina 28584

Available on-line at
http://www.theoutlawsandralove.com

Contact at slppet@yahoo.com

Cover Art by Adam Thompson
www.retrographics.biz

This book is dedicated to my green-eyed woman- my wife Judy, my love of 43 years. Thanks, Hon, for putting up with Kay, Sandra and me this past year. You are the best I've ever known.

TABLE OF CONTENTS

Prologue

On Friday November 21, 1986, at 3:40pm, two men dressed in jeans and sneakers and wearing ski masks entered the First Citizens Bank, in Cape Carteret, North Carolina and fired fourteen rounds into the ceiling destroying the security cameras. One of the men herded the bank employees and customers into a small conference room and kept his automatic weapon trained on them while the other vaulted over the counter and took fourteen hundred from the cash drawers.

As the men were robbing the bank, two young black men who had just cashed their paychecks at the bank raced across the street to the Cape Carteret Police Department and burst in on Officer Joe Willis who was on duty.

"They're robbing the bank!" One of the young men shouted his eyes as big as saucers.

Officer Willis jumped to his feet, "Where?" He asked.

The young men pointed out the window and across Rte 24, "First Citizens! They came in that brown car and we heard them shooting inside the bank!"

Just then, the county 911 office reported a bank robbery alarm from First Citizens Bank had been received on the police radio. Officer Willis shouted as he went out the front door, "Stay here!"

Willis jumped into his patrol car and pulled out onto Rte 24 heading towards the bank. As he approached the bank, a brown 1986 Buick Regal shot out from the

1

parking lot across the highway and headed east on Rte 24. Officer Willis pursued the vehicle for about a half a mile, his lights flashing and siren on, while he reported the pursuit on his radio. Suddenly, the Regal made an abrupt left hand turn across the highway and into a small park on the corner of Rte 24 and Taylor Notion Road. As Officer Willis followed with his siren and blue light flashing, Captain Faron Hill of the Cape Carteret Police Department picked up the 911 call on his scanner. He was off duty and traveling west on Rte 24 in his pickup when he saw Willis turn onto the dirt road that entered the park.

Hill turned right onto the dirt road and into a hail of bullets. The suspects had stopped, jumped out of their car, and opened fire on Officer Willis with two automatic weapons. Captain Hill hit the brakes hard, skidding to a stop behind the patrol car. Both officers returned fire. The suspects jumped back into their car, drove through the park, and out onto Taylor Notion Road heading northwest with both officers in pursuit.

As the officers pursued the suspects, one of the men leaned out the passenger side window and opened fire with a Mini 14. Several bullets hit the patrol car. One of them hit the radar unit mounted on the dash and the fragments from both the unit and the bullet struck Joe Willis in the head and shoulder. The patrol car slowed. At the intersection of Rte 58, the suspects turned right headed northwest. The patrol car pulled off the road and came to a stop.

Captain Hill pulled in behind the patrol car, ran up alongside the car, and looked inside. Officer Joe Willis was slumped on the front seat in a pool of blood.

The Bear Woman

That was the lead story on the news that night as I prepared dinner for Hank and me. "Oh my gosh!" I thought I'd been in the bank that afternoon around 3:30. "Wasn't I lucky?"

The anchor continued the story, Joe Willis had been treated and released from the hospital, and authorities had identified the gunmen as Edwin Pete Black and Michael John Shornock, a graduate of Swansboro High School.

Hank and I had moved to Cape Carteret in 1975. He worked on base at Camp Lejuene and I wrote for the local newspaper when I wasn't working on writing the great American novel.

The lead story on the news a few nights later was a bit more edgy. The two bank robbers had been seen in Edneyville, a small community in western North Carolina. Edwin Pete Black was captured, surrendering to the police without incident, but Michael Shornock escaped following a gun battle with local authorities. As we sat in the living room and watched the story unfold, we learned that Shornock's friends in this area called him 'Rambo' as he was considered an expert in survival skills. This nickname came from his two-year association with a woman that lived on the edge of The Croatan National Forest up Rte 58. Her name was Sandra Horne, but she also, was known as "The Bear Woman" or "The Goat Woman" or "The Snake Lady" depending on who was telling you about her.

"I think we ran a story about her some time ago."

"Yea, her name seems familiar to me," Hank responded as the news continued.

The story changed to a field reporter who had tracked Ms. Horne to her home. He was standing in the forest looking a bit unnerved. He reported that he had interviewed Sandra Horne, but she would not allow him to take any film of her. This reluctance to be photographed caught my attention. I've always been fascinated with unusual people. I am drawn to them as they are drawn to me. Hank feels that I'm somewhat eccentric; I feel he should have his head examined, but it seems to work for the two of us.

The reporter stated that Sandra had offered to help the police by going into the mountains in the Edneyville area, finding Michael Shornock, and talking him into surrendering to the police. She felt she could do this successfully as she claimed to be the one who had taught Shornock about surviving in the wilderness. The police rejected her offer.

"Sorry to see such a young man on the wrong side of the law." Hank commented.

"What do you think about her?" I asked.

"I think she's an oddball alright."

"I'd like to meet her," I responded. My fascination remained intact.

For the next couple of days I thought about Michael Shornock and Sandra Horne. I'll admit being curious about their relationship. I talked to a few friends about 'The Bear Woman' and heard some rather outrageous stories about her. She was everything from a prostitute to a spy for the CIA, she grew up in the South West or Europe, she had been a hunting guide and president of a bank, and she had killed two men. There is never a shortage of stories in the small town south. There was something about her that struck me and that everyone seemed to agree on; she was not a person to be taken lightly. Most of the people I talked to actually warned me to stay away from her, saying she was dangerous.

Well, there's the moth to the flame!

I found out that one of the places she frequented was a small grocery store on Rte 58 named Piner's Store, in Peletier. I stopped by about 2pm in the afternoon and spoke to an older man named Arvis who worked there. He knew Sandra. I was astonished by the stories and how quickly he shared them. I could feel myself being drawn in.

He told me she lived alone in a trailer on a few acres of land up Rte 58 about a mile. I drove by a couple of times. You couldn't see her place from the road, but you could see the path that led back to it. November weather in Carteret County North Carolina runs to the 60's. It was a sunny day, but I'll never forget the feeling I had when I parked my car, walked back the dirt road, and stepped onto the path. Suddenly, the temperature changed. You could feel the coolness of the forest and the silence. I was only a few hundred yards from the highway, but you couldn't hear a car. It was quiet, like death.

"What the hell! I'm creeping myself out!" I thought. I walked down the path a few hundred feet and came to a ridge where the trail led down to a wooden bridge that crossed a small stream and then up to another ridge. I glanced up and could now see the trailer in a clearing in the woods; it looked warm and inviting. The bridge was hand-cut from pine and as I walked down the hill, the bridge smelled as good as it looked. Then I noticed a small sign at the end of the bridge:

Welcome to The Enchanted Forest
If you've been invited, come on in, if not, God help you!

"Okay, I said to myself that seems fair. I need an invitation." I looked down at the ground in front of the bridge and a saw a rather sizable snake curled up a few feet off the path. "Time to go."

******

Hank was pissed!

"Kat, people aren't fooling around about this woman. I've done my own asking around; she's an alcoholic and she ain't right in the head. I talked to Chief Swain. He said that the sheriff will not even take her in jail. A couple a three times a year there are incidents and she has bounced back and forth between the law and the mental health system. Half of his men are afraid of her and you went back into the woods without even telling anyone where you were? What were you thinking?"

"Hank, you're right. When you're right, you're right. I don't know what I was thinking. The forest isn't anything like the neighborhoods I go into when I'm doing a story on a robbery or murder in Jacksonville. Nope, no snakes in those neighborhoods," I hollered into the living room while I loaded the damn dishwasher.

"You're going to do this aren't you?" Hank asked softly.

I turned around. Hank was standing behind me. "I don't know, but if I do, I'll let you know, promise."

The Bear Woman

On Wednesday, November 26, four hundred officers surrounded Michael John Shornock in a rugged stretch of mountains near Edneyville, North Carolina. He shot and wounded two SBI officers, David Wooten and Steele Myers, but he was killed by a single bullet in the head fired by a local police officer. Michael John Shornock was twenty-one years old.

Thursday the 27th was Thanksgiving; we always have a big crowd of family and friends. Sandra was in my mind all day. On Friday, I walked on the beach in Emerald Isle. It was sunny and warm, hitting 70 in the afternoon. Aren't we lucky?" I thought. "We have our health, we have jobs, we live in a beautiful coastal area, and I have Hank. We are truly blessed, but what about others, those less fortunate?" My mind wandered; I wanted the story. I made my decision. Hank and I talked over the weekend.

On Monday morning December 1, I dropped a note to Sandra at Piner's Store. The next few days I stopped by the store each afternoon, nothing. Arvis told me she hadn't been there. On Thursday afternoon, I stopped by late, around 4pm.

"She was here alright!" Arvis announced excitedly. "She left you this note. She sat right over there and wrote it." He pointed at one of the card tables in the store where customers could sit.

"And then she put it back in the envelope and had me scotch tape it for you." He followed.

I opened the note and read it. It was a note from Sandra inviting me to meet at her trailer Friday afternoon at 1pm.

"What's it say?" he asked.

"Honey, if Ms. Horne wanted you to know, she wouldn't have scotch taped the envelope." I smiled and gave him a hug. "Thank you, thanks very much. I won't forget your kindness."

That night Hank and I talked. He didn't like my going to meet Sandra alone, but he understood and we agreed on a time that I needed to be back before he called out the militia. He asked me if I wanted to take a can of pepper spray in my purse, but I declined. At 5'9" and 150 pounds I considered myself big enough to handle most situations should I need to, but to be honest I was a bit nervous about meeting The Bear Woman. Hank had told me that she worked on the docks in Morehead City. There was no doubt in my mind that I was about to meet a formidable woman. I parked my car at the end of the dirt road and, for the second time, walked down the narrow trail that led back to Sandra's trailer.

Again, I felt I was walking away from my world, a world I knew well and into another world that I knew little about. The forecast for Friday was partly cloudy; the part I was in sure was and the woods made everything darker. The dampness in the air filled my nose with the smell of pine. I walked along quietly. Even a novice can do that in a pine forest because of the needle bed on the floor of the forest. Any hunter can tell you that the forest changes with each step you take, so I walked along slowly taking in the changing view. I admit I may have looked behind me or to the sides more often than I normally would. I just didn't want to be surprised by anything jumping out at me. I got to the ridge where I could see the bridge and Sandra's trailer. I walked down to the bridge and stopped. The damn snake was still there.

"You guarding the fort, pal?" I asked the snake somewhat nervously.

"He won't hurt you, honey."

"GEEZZZ!" I jumped, startled by the voice so close behind me.

I spun around and a few feet behind me on the trail stood The Bear Woman, Sandra Horne, all 5'3" and 115 pounds of her!

The first thing I noticed about her was her big green eyes, like a cat, but just beautiful. She had thick reddish-brown hair cut in a boyish shag and her face was quite wrinkled; she wore no makeup. She was dressed in a flannel shirt, jeans, and dirty work boots. A brown floppy hat sat atop her head. She had a double-barreled 16-gauge shotgun in her left hand.

"You look like you've seen a ghost. You okay sweetie?" She asked in a voice that was as eloquent as mine was southern

"This is The Bear Woman?" I thought.

"I-I...where the hell did you come from? You scared the crap out of me."

"I'm Sandra; my guess is you're Kat." She extended her right hand and I reached out and shook it as I nodded affirmatively. It was at that very moment that all doubt I may have had about this old woman standing in front of me was well dispersed. It was like trying to squeeze granite, and while she held my hand in a vice-like grip, her big green eyes stared into my dark brown ones as if she was reading my soul. I had but a single thought; she had no fear.

"Don't worry about him; he won't hurt you unless you step on him." She released her grip and stepped past the snake and me and onto the bridge. "This way, honey."

I followed her across the bridge and as I did, I couldn't help but notice that Sandra had been blessed with that natural wiggle that some women have. There was a butcher-block table outside the trailer. A hose ran from the trailer to the top of the table and was held in place with a pipe clamp. Sandra turned on the water at the side of the trailer and the water began flowing down the table. She unbuttoned her flannel shirt and pulled out a dead gray squirrel. She gutted and skinned the squirrel disposing of the head and entrails in a bucket beside the table. She removed her shirt with as much thought as you'd take off your shoes. She wore no bra. She washed the blood off her well-toned belly. I really couldn't believe that a woman her age had such nice breasts.

"Dinner," she said as she wrapped the squirrel in paper and looked at me with those big green eyes. She smiled. She did have an infectious smile even though her teeth were badly stained, but she had something that shown through, a generousness of spirit. I smiled back.

Sandra put her shirt back on and walked over towards two tree stumps to the right of the trailer. Sitting on top of one of the stumps was a bottle of wine and a single wine glass.

"Have a seat, Kat' and let's talk some."

I sat down on one of the stumps as Sandra opened the wine and poured a glass and handed it to me. I sniffed the wine, swirled it a bit, and took a small sip.

10

As I did, Sandra raised the bottle to her lips and took what I think anyone would say was a long drink. She put the bottle between her legs, took a hard pack of cigarettes out of her shirt pocket, and lit one inhaling it as if it was sweet perfume.

"Ahhh," she sighed. "So you want to write a story about me because you think I'm unusual. I've asked around about you, Kat. People think you may be a bit eccentric yourself."

"You've been talking to my husband haven't you?"

"Har-har...that's funny." She laughed and threw her head back. "That's a knee slapper. I like you already, Kat. Now seriously," and suddenly all the emotion ran away from her face. "You're known around this area, too, with your long dark ponytail and your 60's long dresses, all those earrings, and silver and turquoise rings on every finger. People think you're eccentric; they think I'm crazy. You know the difference, don't you?"

"Not sure I do," I responded.

"Money, honey, money." She took another drink. "Why do you want to write about me?"

"Well, Miss Sandra..."

"Wait a minute, Kat, I'm Sandra. I'm not Miss anybody. How old do you think I am anyway girl?"

"Well, how old are you?" I asked.

"Forty-six."

It actually felt like I had been punched in the stomach. Sandra was a year older than I was! In the south, it's

a bit of tradition that you call an older woman, "Miss"
"What a faux pas!" I thought.

"How old are you, Kat?"

"I-I'm forty-five," I stuttered, "I came up here because
you sounded like a person with an interesting
background."

"Got it, honey. You're looking for my back-story."

"Exactly!" I was a bit surprised Sandra knew the term,
but I was quickly learning that this was not an
individual to underestimate. "Can you tell me anything
about Michael Shornock?"

"Well, I can tell you he was an angry young man, with
good cause."

"What do you mean?"

"He was raped while he was in jail. It's the reason he
swore he'd never return."

"Were you lovers?"

"Kat, I don't talk much about my men. Michael was
here for a while after he got out of prison. We had
known each other for more than two years. We spent
a lot of time together; I taught him many things about
living in the wilderness. His death was needless."

Sensing her stress, I said, "I've heard some things
about you since the robbery. How did you get all
those nicknames?"

 "Well, hunters call me "The Bear Woman" because in
addition to getting my limit of deer each hunting
season, I always bag a bear. "

The Bear Woman

"I've also been called "The Goat Woman" because all the jobs I do are dirty. I spray paint and drywall, do concrete work and stucco and I'm a fair hand at carpentry and plumbing. I hunt, fish, shrimp, crab, clam, oyster, and take care of animals. I spend all my money on my animals. Well, almost all of it."

Sandra raised the bottle and took another drink.

"Something that's told of me that isn't true; I do bathe every day and wash my hair. Oh, one other thing, I do own two goats." Sandra winked at me. I liked her sense of humor.

"And the name 'Snake Lady'?"

"The local children started calling me that because I keep snakes as pets. I have some background in snake handling. If the kids find a snake, they'll bring it over and I'll let it stay. They're free to slither at will on my property. If you don't bother them, they won't bother you."

"I've heard that you have a lot of animals on your property. How many do you have and where are they?"

"I have a compound for them behind the trailer. I have thirty-one animals, but that's not counting the snakes or the three-legged black bear I call Peg Leg. He's escaped hunters for the last three years now. Come hunting season, he packs in on my property. I feed him meat scraps from the butcher. He's never threatened any of my animals. I have more dogs than any other animal. I have coon dogs, deer dogs, duck dogs, and a few nothing dogs who just eat and scratch fleas. I also have four cats. I have a few geese, several ducks, and lots of chickens. I have two silly goats, named "Sugar Pie" and "Bambi". "Bambi" is really special. He looked like Bambi all right when I first got him. His mother rejected him, so I fed him for six months, milk and molasses, on a stoop at the entrance to the little house I built for him. All goats like stoops to get in and out of their houses. Every night I held him in my arms and rocked him to sleep. Now "Bambi" weighs a hundred twenty pounds. He still wants to get rocked to sleep in my lap. So, we made a deal; no bottle, but some nights I still sit on the stoop with his head tucked under my arm and pet him until he goes to sleep. Do you have any animals, Kat?"

"Whoa," I thought. This is way beyond being an animal lover. This is someone who needs to love and be loved. "We have a cat named 'Naughty Kitty;' if you met him, you'd understand the name."

"What a great name that is!" Sandra smiled and then lifted her bottle up again. We sat there and talked for a while. Sandra finished the bottle and I nursed my glass while she was drinking.

"I want to tell you my story, Kat. I think it would be good for some folks to hear it. One thing I will tell you now, you've never heard anything like it before."

"Well, why don't we try a few meetings and see how it goes."

"But I want to tell the story the way I want to tell it. I don't want to answer a lot of questions and have to explain a lot of things to you. We come from different worlds, Kat." Sandra's voice began to fade a bit as the wine took its effect.

"Okay Sandra, how's this sound? I'll bring a tape recorder with me and you just talk. When you're done,

I'll come get it, write up the session, and give you a copy to read and comment on, and then you can decide what you'd like to cover the next time. How does tomorrow at 10am sound? "

"I like that." Sandra responded. "Tomorrow at 10am, deal." She extended her right hand, and I shook her hand; it felt like Jell-O.

Chicago

"I feel I should tell you something about my past. Not to get any sympathy, mind you, but to let you know where I'm coming from.

I was born Sandra Love Christensen in Chicago on May 15, 1940, to what you'd think of as an upper middle class family. When I was five years old, my parents divorced and my father, who was a banker, remarried. My father visited me regularly at first. Together we made stick soldiers, drew cartoons, and played with toy animals. When his new wife started having children, his visits became less frequent and I missed him very much.

My mother remarried in 1949. As a result, we moved from an apartment in a middle class neighborhood to a seedy section of Chicago where my stepfather, who was a cab driver, owned a small house. Suddenly, at age nine, I saw a different side of life: drugs, drinking, gangs, and prostitutes. It didn't take me long to learn what was going on in the neighborhood. I became streetwise fast.

I got along pretty well with my stepfather. He took me fishing, to the park, and even called me his 'little boy.' We started getting into arguments after I started dating, I was fourteen, but I matured early. He caught me making out with my first boyfriend on the sofa one evening when he got off work early. My blouse was off and he bellowed and called me a whore as he chased my boyfriend out of the house. I was so embarrassed at the way my stepfather reacted, I cried myself to sleep. My mother, who was a nurse, was still at work. One day my mother asked me why I argued so much with my stepfather and I told her. Again, I was hurt because my own mother sided with my stepfather. I guess I lost respect for my parents and I suppose all adults. I decided from then on, I would make my own decisions and live with them right or wrong.

I became headstrong. I hated school; it was boring. Both my parents were now working at night so I came and went as I pleased. My grades were always good, mostly A's. I didn't study much, didn't have to.

On a warm summer night shortly after my fifteenth birthday, I had been hanging out with some friends and was on my way home around 11pm. I passed Shorty's, the bar at the end of our street. There were some men and women outside laughing, drinking beer, and smoking cigarettes. I could smell the acrid smoke as I approached the group and heard the bebop music coming from inside. As I passed them on the sidewalk, I noticed one of the men was very good looking. He had dark hair, blue eyes, one of those square cut jaws, and he was very tan. He was standing alone on the far side of the group leaning against the wall. He didn't look much older than most of my friends except he wore slacks and dress shoes, had a gold watch, and his body was very muscular. He was smoking and drinking a beer. Our eyes met and I smiled at him.

"Hey," he said softly.

"Hey, yourself," I responded. I slowed, but didn't stop.

"My name is Brad," he said gently as he walked up behind me.

I turned to my right as he came abreast of me. "I'm Sandra." What a great smile he had!

"Where're you going?"

"Headed home."

"Oh, you got a curfew eh?"

"No, I don't have a curfew thank you." That miffed me a bit.

"Great. Come on, you can hang out with us for awhile."

"And do what?"

"Have a beer. Come on, I'll buy you a drink. Get a chance to talk, get to know you Sandra. You can tell me where you got those big green eyes." He smiled again. So did I.

"Sure, why not."

"Okay. Stay here and I'll be right back."

I leaned up against the wall and propped my foot up behind me. In a few minutes, Brad came back with a bottle of beer and I had my first drink. It was pretty good on a hot summer night and I was feeling grown up.

"How old are you?" He asked.

"Eighteen." I lied. "How old are you?"

"Thirty, today. It's my birthday."

We must have talked for an hour. He asked me a lot about myself and bought me two more beers. Damn, I felt important. Around midnight one of the other men came over and Brad introduced me to his friend, Clint. He was a much bigger man, nice enough, but he seemed to be in a hurry to leave. Around 12:15, Brad told me he was leaving, and then he asked me for my telephone number and I gave it to him. He repeated it again and again, screwing it up each time and both of us laughed. Clint pulled up in a car.

"I got to go Sandra with the big green eyes," he said.

"Happy birthday!" I said and wrapped my arms around his neck and kissed him.

"Wow, girl, you are a good kisser!" He smiled. "I have no idea what your number is after that." He opened the back door of the car and swept his hand like a chauffeur might. "Hop in and we'll make sure you get home safe. Then I'll know where you live."

I got in.

I remember Brad kissing me and unbuttoning my shirt. My heart raced as I felt him climb on top of me in the back seat. I remember the passion, the innocence, and the car stopping on the side of the road.

"I got to take a leak," Clint said as he got out.

Suddenly, the back door flew open and there was Clint. The big burley man pulled me out of the car and dragged me by my hair out into a field.

"Let go of me you bastard!" I screamed. "Brad, help me please!"

Out in the middle of a cow pasture Clint pulled me up and turned me around as I dug my nails into the hand that was pulling my hair. Clint pulled his right hand back and smacked me hard across the face. It felt like my head exploded. I felt hands ripping my blouse down from behind. I felt my bra unclasp and I tried to kick Clint, but he moved and then he slapped me again harder than I have ever been hit. I saw stars. I felt weak. My left eye was puffing up, my skirt, and panties were being pulled off. Next, Clint was on top of me, and then he was inside me. I was scared and started to cry.

"Shut up you little bitch or I'll beat the shit out of you!" He hollered.

I didn't make any more noise as they took turns raping me for the next three hours.

When they were through, they left me on the side of the road holding my clothes. As they drove off, I read the license plate number and committed it to memory by singing it over and over again, as I dressed and dragged myself out of the cow pasture. Several cows were in the pasture and I could see them in the moonlight. It was the first time I'd seen cows except on cowboy shows on television. That night was the first time for a lot of things.

I was exhausted, angry, and dirty, but I managed to walk eight miles that night to a police station, report the rape, and give them a description and license plate number. They caught the two men and I testified in court at their trial. They were both recent parolees and they were both given life sentences. I remember at the sentencing Brad looked different, not as handsome as I remembered, but Clint was just as big. This was the third time that a man who I had feelings for let me down.

As the legal mess was being straightened out, my mother and stepfather tried to get me to go to public school again but I refused. The way the boys looked at me, it made me uncomfortable. In the end, my real father paid for me to attend a private school. It turned out to be a richer version of public school and somehow the kids had found out about my past. I quit school at sixteen and never completed high school.

I began working as a waitress. It gave me something to do and I've always enjoyed helping people. I worked in a diner for about four months. One of the customers that I'd call a 'regular' owned a bar and strip club called The Coral Club. His name was Pete Contino. Pete was in his sixties, short and stocky with curly salt and pepper hair and black Clark Kent glasses. He always wore a suit and never wore a tie, just a dress shirt that showed off the gold chain he wore around his neck. He also wore two diamond rings and a gold watch. I remember the night we talked he asked me to sit down in his booth.

"How would you like to come and work for me at the club?"

I smiled at him. "That's nice of you to offer me a job. Why are you asking me?"

"Because you're pretty and I like the way you interact with the customers here. You'll make more money in my club in one night than you'll make here in a week."

"That sounds good. What would I have to do for this money?" I asked.

Pete smiled. "You're a smart girl Sandra." He leaned forward in the booth and lowered his voice. "Listen to me carefully now. I know what happened to you. Nothing like that will ever happen to you if you work in my club, understand?" Pete talked with his hands as well as his mouth. "If you have a problem, you come to me, and I make the problem go away, you follow?"

"I'm not twenty-one."

"That's not a problem," Pete said as he began to eat his breakfast.

"I'd like to think about it."

"Sure, take your time, ask around. Let me know what you decide."

So, I asked some of the girls I worked with about him. They told me that he had connections with the Italian mob in Chicago, but he was a standup guy and they thought he liked me. I started to work in The Coral Club that weekend. The first customers I had tipped me twenty dollars. Pete was right. It was good money.

I worked in the club for a couple of weeks before I met Frank Tangredi. He was a tall, good-looking, twenty-eight year old Italian man that oozed charm. Every girl in the bar was in love with him. They all thought he looked like a young Dean Martin.

One night while I was waiting at the bar for some drinks, Frank came in and sat down at the end of the bar. He ordered his drink and turned towards me.

"Hi, I'm Frank Tangredi." He extended his hand.

I reached out to shake his hand, but instead he held my hand with his thumb across my fingers and his fingers under my palm. He bent his head and gently kissed my hand. The heat began somewhere below my waist and rose until it reached the top of my head. No one had ever done that to me before.

"Well, aren't you the charmer," I managed as the bartender brought my drinks over. I put the drinks on my serving tray and as I turned to leave, "I'm Sandra." Then, I gave him a smile as gentle as his kiss.

As I was serving my customers, one of the other waitresses, an older woman named Connie, caught my eye and her dark eyes widened as she cocked her head in Frank's direction. I turned away fast and blushed. When I turned around Pete was standing next to Frank with his arm around his shoulder. Their two heads weren't more than an inch apart. Pete was talking and Frank was listening. His head was nodding affirmatively. By the time I got back to the bar, Pete was talking to a group of men that had just come in. Frank turned towards me.

"I hope you weren't offended with the kiss, Sandra. I apologize if you were."

"Not at all, Frank." I smiled and he seemed to relax. We talked the whole evening while I worked. Four other men joined Frank at a table and I waited on them. At the end of the night, they tipped me a hundred dollars. The next night Frank came in again and eventually asked me out. We began dating.

Most of what I know about sex and men, Frank taught me. He was an excellent, considerate lover. Practiced and patient, he thought of sex as an art form, and a woman's body was his canvas. Before long, I got pregnant; I was seventeen. He was very worried about the pregnancy; all I thought about was Pete and the statement he had made about making problems disappear. I was in love with Frank and I was afraid Pete would have Frank killed.

We talked and Frank arranged an abortion. Abortions were not legal in 1957, but Frank had connections. Afterwards, I remember the nurse finishing up. I felt a wet, warm, flowing sensation under my lower back. I reached down and my hand came up covered in blood. The nurse inserted a large cotton pad into my vagina and sent me home with pain medication and more pads. Frank looked very worried and offered to stay with me. I reminded him that my mother was a nurse and told him I'd be fine.

Frank dropped me at the house and I called off work and went to bed. My mother asked me what was wrong, and I told her I was having menstrual cramps. I don't think she believed me, but what could she do.

I was fine in a few days and returned to work. The second night I was at the club Frank came in. During one of the breaks, he grabbed me and sat me up on the bar. He got down on one knee, reached in his pocket, and pulled out a diamond ring. There were about thirty customers and another dozen staff in the club; you could hear a pin drop.

"Sandra, my green-eyed lady, I do love you so. Would you do me the honor of being my wife?"

I was stunned. Tears welled up in my eyes as I shook my head up and down vehemently. Frank put the ring on my finger, and I jumped off the bar and into his arms as everyone began applauding and the dancers on stage whooped it up like it was a ball game. Then I got a hug from everyone in the bar; Pete was last. He held me close and whispered in my ear, "When you tell your folks, tell them the wedding is already paid for."

"How...?"

"A gift from my daughter." He kissed me on the forehead.

Later, Connie told me that Pete's only child, his daughter, had died of cancer twenty years earlier. She was seventeen.

The Outlaw Sandra Love

I was eighteen when I married Frank. I had been
married about three months when I got pregnant
again. I stopped work and became a housewife. Frank
had a consulting business and often was out until the
wee hours of the morning entertaining clients, so the
story went. What angered me the most was his
lateness or not calling at all when I had prepared
dinner. I told him over and over, "I don't care where
you are or what you're doing, just call me, and let me
know if you're going to be late, or if you're not coming
home for dinner."

I soon realized it might have not been such a good
idea to marry a 'lady's man.' In the seventh month of
my pregnancy, the doctor told me that the thick foul-
smelling vaginal discharge I had was caused by
Gonorrhea, a venereal disease commonly known as
'the clap'. My philandering husband had brought the
disease home. This not only endangered my health,
but the health of my baby. The doctor put me on an
antibiotic. I put Frank on notice.

Shortly before my baby's birth, Frank and I had a
terrible argument, he left. I was sad. My son Anthony
Tangredi was born on September 19, 1959. I was
nineteen and alone. Frank refused to pay child
support, and I wouldn't tell Pete any of this. I was
afraid he would have Frank killed. We had no
electricity and very little food or clothing. When my
stepfather heard about the situation, he asked me to
come back home.

I thought, "He's being so nice, maybe he's trying to
make amends for the way he treated me when I was
fourteen." I accepted his offer and moved back home.

During the next two years, I worked at The Coral
Club mostly on the days my mother had off. She liked

to care for Anthony. Frank and I divorced and I never saw him in the club. Pete died of a massive heart attack and the club transferred ownership and management. I was a popular waitress and dated a few of the men who frequented the club, but my main man was my little Tony.

Then one night I came home and no one was there. Tony was not in his bed and neither my mother nor stepfather was home. I was in a panic. Had Frank done something to them? Was there trouble in the neighborhood? Had something happened to my little Tony? I looked around the house for a note, anything... nothing. I was on my way to the front door and the neighbors when the phone rang.

"Hello?"

"Honey, it's me, mom."

"Mom, where are you? Is everything okay? Is Tony hurt?"

"We're at the hospital."

"What's wrong, mom?"

"It's Tony; he had some sort of seizure. He's fine, but he's going to have to stay for awhile for observation. Your stepfather is on his way to pick you up; he should be there in a few minutes."

"Mom!" I was in tears."

"Be strong Sandra. Now is the time when you must be strong for your child."

"Is he going to be alright?"

"We'll have to wait and see. The doctors will be performing some tests in the next few days and I'm sure they'll get to the bottom of this real soon. Can you be strong for that long Sandra?"

"Yes, yes, I will mom, I will."

"Good. I'll see you in a little while then."

My mother hung up the phone and I sat down and started to cry. Then I stopped. I began to feel angry. I went to the kitchen and dried my eyes, blew my nose and threw some water on my face. Then, I got real angry.

I paced the floor for a few minutes, but it seemed like hours. I remembered when my father left and me and my mom were all alone. I remembered her strength. I swore to God I would be strong for Tony.

My stepfather drove me to the hospital and I practically ran to Tony's room. It was late and I think if it hadn't been for my mother being a nurse there, I wouldn't have been able to see him. I opened his door quietly.

"Mom."

"Hi honey. How are you doing?"

"My head hurts a bit and I'm thirsty."

"I'll take care of that," my mom said as she turned and left the room.

I sat down on the bed and leaned over and hugged my little guy. "It will be fine, just fine now."

The next day several specialists saw Tony and ordered many tests. Eventually, we found out that Tony had CAE, Childhood Absence Epilepsy; possibly brought on by the VD I had while I was pregnant since we could not establish any family history. The doctors said he had not suffered any damage, as these were not grand mal seizures, but the frequency and repetitiveness of the seizures would require expensive medicine, close observation, and occasionally hospitalization.

The next few months were an ordeal, more seizures, more doctors, and more bills. I was going deeper and deeper into debt and I knew I'd have to find some way of handling the cost of Tony's treatment before I went bust.

One night I was in the club and Connie and I were talking. She told me that she couldn't recommend becoming a stripper because they don't make much more than we did. I told her I wasn't sure I'd be any good at it, it's more than just taking off your clothes, it's knowing how to dance and show off your body.

A big man named Grayson was sitting at the bar and he must have overheard our conversation. He waved a twenty at me and I walked over.

"How are you doing tonight Grayson? Can I get you something?"

He dropped the twenty down between my breasts. The short cocktail dresses we wore showed enough cleavage that it wasn't hard to do.

"I'm good thanks Sandra, but maybe there's something I can do for you."

"What's that, Grayson?"

"If its money you need, I could get you a job in Gary, Indiana and you'd make a lot more than you make here and pay no taxes."

"How much do you think I make here, Grayson?"

"Fifty, would be a good night wouldn't it?"

"Well, you're in the ballpark. And what would that job be?" I asked.

"You'd entertain men for money, just like here."

"Are we talking about prostitution, Grayson?"

"That's your word Sandra, but you could earn two or three times more than you do here and not pay taxes. You'll make more than that if you're willing to do the unusual."

"Well, I do need the money. My son has been hospitalized several times because of frequent seizures and I don't have any insurance. I don't qualify for welfare because I have a job. You can imagine how much I owe in hospital bills. If I can't pay them down a bit, I'm afraid he may not get the best treatment."

"Look Sandra, I've known you awhile. You're a good girl in my book. You're in a tough jam and you need money fast. Most of these guys are looking for sex and some company and they will pay well for it. Guess the question is, are you strong enough to take a job like that for awhile?"

"I'll let you know. I need to think it over."

"I'll be in town until Friday."

Chicago

Being a prostitute wasn't one of my life's ambitions, but I knew I couldn't make five hundred to a thousand a week doing anything else. Then I thought of my mother's words, "Can you be strong?"

For my Tony, I'd sleep with the devil himself.

The Outlaw Sandra Love

Working For The Outfit

Gary, Indiana is in Lake County, which borders Illinois. The town abuts Chicago's city line, and is considered part of the Chicago metropolitan area. So when I told Grayson Toth that I'd try it for a while, I wasn't moving away just working in the next town over.

My story is not going to be a tutorial on how to become a prostitute. It is also not going to be me telling you how good I was and it's not going to be filled with steamy sex, because steamy sex is not what you have with a prostitute. Steamy sex is what you have with your lover. Prostitutes perform a service; we're part of the oldest service industry in the world. If you're good, you create a fantasy that is unattainable anywhere else, but this is not a business with more than one measure of success. The measure is always, how much money did you make?

I started in a cafe that was on the ground floor of a hotel owned by the mob. You couldn't tell that unless you worked there because everything from the deed to the license to the federal tax returns was in someone else's name, but the mob owned it, we all knew that.

Grayson ran the place; he was my first customer. I was twenty-one years old. He taught me what was expected of the girls; time and money, customer service and security. He was a big man and very strong, and he showed me ways to disable a man very quickly if a customer became aggressive or assaultive. Grayson had grown up in Kentucky and had wrestled in high school. He had been a Marine in

33

World War II and had taught self-defense courses. I took a great deal of interest in this and practiced with Grayson once a week in the basement of the hotel where he worked out. I remember thinking, "If I had only known this when I was raped."

Grayson introduced me to the other girls who were all older and each one had some advice or story they shared with me. After the second day, Grayson took me up to one of the rooms. On the way up in the elevator he said, "Today we're going to role play. Here's the key to the room. When the elevator doors open, you're on. I'm the John." John is a term used to describe a prostitute's customer. It comes from "John Doe" and the desire to remain anonymous. Grayson was deadly serious and I realized my training was over. The doors opened, I stepped out and turned around.

"This way, honey." I smiled. I felt like I was an actress.

I walked down the hall, opened the door to the room, turned on the light and Grayson stepped in. I closed the door behind him, walked over to the table lamp, and turned it on. Then I looked over my shoulder and asked, "Would you like to do this?" I put my right hand on the zipper of the little black dress I was wearing. When you put your hand in the middle of your back, it makes your boobs jut out. I remember all the strippers at The Coral Club had that move.

"Sure." Grayson came over and pulled the zipper down; the dress dropped to the floor. I turned around and stood in front of him wearing black panties, black heels, and a smile.

"Damn you have some big breasts for such a little girl." He practically gasped.

"Thank you, now what can I do for you tonight?"

"Let's fuck!" Grayson came towards me, but I held up my hand and kept him at arm's length.

"That sounds like fun, but before that happens there are two things we need to take care of first."

"Oh yea..."

"You're going to put a hundred dollars on that table and then I'm going to help you undress and wash up a bit."

"Is that so? And what if I don't want to do that?" Grayson was testing me.

"What's your name honey?" I tried to distract him, just like I would with little Tony when he got fixated on something he shouldn't have been doing.

"Grayson," he told me.

"Listen to me carefully, Grayson. The men who own this hotel insist that business be conducted in a certain way; it protects their assets. If we can't do that, then you have to leave, but I'd rather you'd stay."

"And who's going to make me leave? You, little girl?"

"Grayson, if I scream men will come through that door and you won't like what will happen and I won't see you again."

"You don't think anyone can hear you six floors below us do you?"

"What makes you think anyone is six floors below us?"

Grayson smiled, "Okay honey." He reached in his pocket and pulled out a lot of money. He rolled a single one hundred dollar bill off and put it on the table.

From that point on, Grayson was the perfect John. He told me what he wanted and I gave it to him. Grayson was a big man and when he was on top of me, I felt warm and secure like being wrapped in a blanket. He made me climax. When we were finished, we dressed and he turned to me saying, "You were great honey. If I want to ask for you next time, what's your name?"

"M-my name, my name is Sandra, Sandra Love." I was not prepared for the question and so I just blurted out my first and middle names.

"What a great name. Keep that." He told me as we left the room.

"Okay," I thought.

We went down to the cafe and sat at one of the tables. Grayson critiqued me.

"Sandra, you were great. You're a natural. You could do very well in this business. You'll make even more money than you thought, but you need to remember three things. First, you owe the house twenty-five dollars.

"And?"

"You kiss great, but don't ever kiss Johns on the mouth; offer your neck."

"Thank you. And the last one?"

"When you fake your orgasm in the future, you can tone it down a bit."

"Okay. All good tips," I smiled. I never saw any reason to tell Grayson the truth.

I worked in the hotel for about six months. My mother was now working day shifts so there was no problem with Tony. I learned a lot and made a lot and Grayson seemed happy. I began buying Tony's medication and paying down some of the hospital bills. Grayson taught me how to drive a car and helped me get my license. I bought a car and I didn't have to take cabs or buses anymore. It was a 1959 Chevy Impala, with the winged tail fins, black and white with a red interior. I thought it was so cool. On my days off, I could take Tony to the park or shopping, but the seizures continued and I worried about my little guy.

One evening when I came into work, there were two men standing in front of the hotel entrance. One of them asked me, "Are you Sandra Love?"

"Yes."

The other man opened the door for me.

I went inside and the lobby was completely empty. Grayson was standing by the counter and called me over.

"Sandra, you've done very well. There is a man here who has heard some good things about you and he wants to meet you. He's in the cafe. You can go in."

"Who is he Grayson, am I in any trouble?" I got real nervous.

Grayson smiled, "No honey, you're not in any trouble. Just the opposite, this is the real deal Sandra. He's the boss, understand?"

"Yes, but..."

"No buts, honey, just be yourself and be respectful."
He waved his hand at me motioning towards the cafe.
"Go!"

I tried to read Grayson's face; he looked a bit tense,
but I didn't think he'd lie to me. The lobby was silent
and dark. Even Danny, the night clerk, wasn't behind
the marble counter where you checked in. All the
couches were empty and there was just the light
coming through the two stained glass doors from
inside the café. I walked towards the doors. I opened
one and went in.

Two more men stood inside; one asked, "Are you
Sandra Love?"

"Yes." It was all I could get out.

"This way, please."

I followed him over to a booth in the corner that I
thought was empty until I was almost alongside it.
Then I saw and smelled the cigar smoke.

"Boss, this is Sandra Love."

An older man with thin graying hair looked up at me.
He stood up and extended his hand.

"Lovely. You are quite beautiful, my dear. My name is
Sam. Will you have a drink with me?"

His deep gravelly voice was powerful, yet polite.

"Thank you, Sam." I sat down in the booth.

"What would you like to drink?"

"Vodka and tonic, please...hold the vodka."

Sam smiled, "Two, thanks Al."

We talked for about an hour. He asked me a lot of questions about my life and I told him the truth. I remember when I told him about something, he'd always ask how I felt about that when it happened, or what did I learn from that experience. He complimented me on everything from my eyes to my eveningwear. He even asked me to tell him a joke, so I did.

"A very old man walked into a brothel and up to the desk where the madam stood. She looked up and asked, 'Can I help you sir?' The elderly gentleman said, 'I'd like a woman for the night.' The madam looked at the old man and asked, 'How old are you pop?' 'Ninety-three,' he responded. The madam questioned him, 'Pop, don't you think you've had it?' The old man responded, 'Oh, I'm sorry. How much do I owe you?'"

Sam laughed. "I like you, Sandra, you've got style. Your joke was on subject, but not vulgar. I'd like to offer you a different position than what you're doing now."

"That sounds interesting. What would I be doing in this position?" I asked.

"You would be doing what you do now, but you would be working in a very expensive apartment in Chicago, all expenses paid. You would be making five hundred with a 75/25 split. There are many other benefits, if you are interested."

"Has Grayson told you that I'm only doing this until my son's medical bills are paid for? I'd like to do other things with my life after that."

"That's good. I have three daughters and they all want careers, too. When you're done, you're done."

"I'd like some time to think it over. Can I let you know by the end of the week?"

"You take your time, ask around, and tell Grayson when you've decided."

Sam and I spent the next two hours together. He was very complimentary. He reminded me of Pete, but obviously, he had more power. He left and when I returned to the café, Grayson and all the girls were sitting at a big round table in the back. The girls got up and ran over to me like I had just hit a walk-off homerun. I could feel my head starting to puff up.

"What did he say Sandra? Where are you going? How much?" The questions flew out of their mouths.

"I guess I've done okay?" I replied. I asked Grayson if I could tell the girls, and he nodded. I showed them the five hundred in my purse. They all squealed, so I gave them the run down. Everyone told me how lucky I was, that my life was going to be so different. I didn't understand why they were so upset when I told them that I had told Sam that I'd like to think about it.

One of the girls, Beverly, advised me, "Do what's right for you, honey."

I took her advice. Two weeks later, I was a call girl for the Chicago mob.

As I found out, The Chicago Mob, The Chicago Mafia, and The Chicago Syndicate are all names for a crime organization more commonly referred to as The Chicago Outfit. Founded in the early 1900's, it grew most famously under Al Capone and his successor, Frank Nitty, during Prohibition. The Outfit was viewed as separate from the five New York mafia families portrayed in "The Godfather" movie.

The Outfit, welcomed any enterprise that brought money into the mob, but there were the seven sisters, the big producers: protection and extortion, prostitution, alcohol and drugs, gambling, theft, loan sharking, and union corruption. Historically, violence and murder were used to eliminate competition or punish those who violated the rules, threatened the organization, or disrespected it. Civilians were considered out of bounds.

During the next three years, I worked as a call girl for The Outfit and enjoyed a standard of living that most girls just dream about, but the lifestyle I cannot recommend. Yes, I paid off all my debt to the hospitals and doctors, I paid for all of Tony's health needs as well as his attendance in a private school, and I lived in one of the nicest apartments in Chicago on Lakeshore Drive overlooking Lake Michigan. Yes, I had money, clothes, jewelry, and cars. I ate well, traveled extensively, started smoking, and became an alcoholic.

Did you think there wasn't a price paid?

In 1965, Tony was in first grade and I felt myself going downhill I needed a way out. I wanted to do more with my life than be a prostitute no matter how good I was at my trade. I had put money aside, about forty thousand dollars. One night when I saw Sam, I told him. We were in a restaurant called The London House.

"Sam, I want to tell you something that's very important."

"What, you need money?"

"No, I have put some aside."

"For what?" He looked up.

"I'm done. I can't do this anymore. I want out."

He pushed his food aside and finished his glass of wine. "Do you know what you're going to do?"

"I'm going back to school. I always was a pretty good student. I want a new start."

"You know how I'll miss you."

"You have been very kind, thank you."

We talked for ten or fifteen minutes more, and then Sam said, "I have a meeting. Al will take you home. You can stay in the apartment until the end of the month."

He pushed his chair back and stood up. I got up as fast as I could and hugged him around the neck, but he wouldn't hug me back. I started to cry and he pulled my arms from around his neck. Everyone in the restaurant was looking. He leaned forward and kissed me on the cheek.

"When you're done, you're done. Be strong."

"My mother's words," I thought. Then he walked out. I never saw him again.

The Offer

I moved to Gary that summer. Several months later, on a Saturday morning, I met Captain John Paul Fulcher for the second time. He worked for the Gary, Indiana police vice squad. The first time we met, I was working at the hotel and he busted me for prostitution. The judge threw the case out. The second time I met him, I was shopping in a grocery store with Tony. Our eyes met as we both reached for a box of Sugar Corn Pops.

"I know you; you're Sandra, Sandra Lov...Sandra T-Tangredi."

Paul was a tall dark-haired man with deep blue eyes. He was one of the most honest police officers I ever met.

"You're Captain Fulcher. I remember you."

"And who is this handsome young man?"

"This is my son, Anthony. Anthony, this is Captain Fulcher. He's a police officer."

Paul was dressed in bell-bottom jeans, sneakers, and a Chicago Bears sweatshirt.

"It's nice to meet you." Tony stuck out his hand and shook Paul's hand. "Are you a Bears fan, too?" he asked.

"Yes, I am!" Paul grinned. "You are very grown-up."

"Thank you," my little guy responded smartly.

We started talking and I learned he was bringing up three children alone because his wife was in a mental hospital. He asked me out, and shortly after our meeting, we began dating. I told Paul that I had left 'the life' and was planning to go back to school. He seemed genuinely happy for me.

My life in Gary settled into a comfortable routine. I had talked to a friend of mine, an attorney, about returning to school. She had advised me to take the GED test and then the SAT's to apply to a college. I studied a book on how to take the GED test, kept house, saw to Tony's needs, and dated Paul. We socialized with his married friends who were nice, but I had absolutely nothing in common with them. Paul was ten years older than me and a rather conservative man considering it was 1966. He insisted that I tone down what I wore since most of my wardrobe was designer clothing. I began to feel like an old woman and I was only in my mid-twenties. We really had a nice thing going, but compared to my former lifestyle, it was too pat, too square, and too boring.

Meanwhile, Tony had started second grade in public school and right away, there were problems. He had a seizure in school and I had to explain his medical condition to the school principal. They told me his attention span was very short, and by age eight, he was falling behind. In spite of the fact that Tony had scored in the gifted range on group I.Q. tests, he was failing in school. The biggest complaint from his teacher was that he didn't pay attention. I met with the school.

"I don't understand. He has a high I.Q. and he did very well last year in school, yet he is failing here. What do you think is the problem?"

The Offer

"Perhaps you could help him with his school work," the principal suggested.

"I do help him. We spend at least an hour a night on homework. Are his homework grades bad?" I asked the teacher, Mrs. Stewart, a woman who was well past sixty.

"No, they're good. But he has a very short attention span and is disruptive in class."

"Are his tests alright?" I asked.

"I think his problem may have something to do with his seizures," Mrs. Stewart responded rather coldly.

I looked over at the principal; he had his head bowed and his face buried in his right hand. It was my first experience with prejudice and I didn't like it. Later, I met with the principal one-on-one. I asked if he could place Tony in the other second grade class. He was sympathetic, but didn't feel that would solve the problem, so, I asked him point blank, "What would you recommend here, Mr. Woods?"

He responded, "His first grade record looked good. Perhaps Anthony might do better in a different environment."

I took Mr. Woods' recommendation and enrolled Tony in the local Catholic school the following week. I asked him to tell Mrs. Stewart that I was sorry Tony's seizures disrupted her class. I was furious, but I had learned to keep my cool.

Tony's new teacher was Sister Mary Elizabeth who was my age. We hit it off from the start. Tony settled down and did very well in the Catholic school. Sister and I stayed in close touch and if anything unusual happened, she told me. Also, whenever possible, I helped with school activities to raise money for the school. I passed the GED test and spent the rest of my time studying for the SAT's. I took the test in the spring of 1966 and scored high enough to enroll at Valparaiso. I started classes in the fall of 1966.

I enjoyed the campus life and the younger students. I started dressing down a bit, wearing mostly jeans and casual tops. I partied with the students on campus and in the fraternities every once in a while, mostly when Tony was with my mom and stepfather. I met many new friends. In the summer of 1969, I realized I was going to be short of money for my senior year tuition. Tony's tuition at Catholic school was not in my original budget. I had taken out all my student loans and would not be able to pay for the last semester. I also was a month behind on the rent.

I went back to work, freelancing from a bar near campus. In four months, I had the money I needed and paid for my spring semester. Just before Christmas though, I was arrested for solicitation. Somehow, Paul had gotten wind of my extracurricular activities and sent an undercover officer in with a tape recorder. Needless to say, we stopped seeing each other, but I was in deep trouble. If the school found out, they could throw me out and a conviction for solicitation might lead not only to jail time, but also to my losing Tony. My future job prospects suddenly dimmed.

"Stupid, stupid, stupid!" I beat myself up for a couple of days and then I called my attorney friend, Jacqueline Kramer, a lawyer, Grayson used. She had a specialized law practice. We met in her office in the Board of Trade Building on Jackson.

"Come in, Sandra, how are you doing? How's that little guy of yours?"

Jackie had one of the biggest offices I had ever seen. She had a gorgeous view of the downtown Chicago canyon seen through a bank of floor-to-ceiling windows behind her desk.

"He's doing very well, thanks." Jackie and I talked for an hour, the first half an hour was catching up, as I hadn't seen her in nearly four years. I asked about Sam. Her response was, "Sam's gone honey. There's a lot of turnover in that job. Now, how can I help you?"

I told her about Paul and about what had happened. I told her about my financial situation and the concerns I had about the University. I told her I'd kill before I'd lose Tony. When I was done, she got up from her desk and walked around to the front of it, and leaned back onto the desk. I remember that dark navy blue pinstripe suit and the white low-cut blouse she wore under it. It showed off her figure well. Considering the quality of the leather shoes, the gold watch, and the diamond earrings, at forty-four years old Jackie was just a class act. I could smell her No. 5.

Jackie looked down at me, frowned, and then asked, "You went to college to get stupid? Why would you do something like that?"

"Tony," I responded softly, and my eyes began to water. "Please, Jackie, help me."

I remember her face changing, softening She stared at me for a while and then spoke, "I'll take care of it."

I stood up. "Thank you." We hugged. "I don't have any money now, but..."

"No charge, Sandra. Maybe sometime you can do a favor for me."

I knew what that meant. As I rode down in the elevator, I felt like I had just made a deal with the devil.

Jackie filed as my attorney of record and I had a preliminary hearing. A court date was set for July. I remember being relieved that I was going to graduate two months before the trial would take place. I had no idea then that neither of those events would ever happen.

In April of 1970, I was nine credits away from graduation. I had a Business Strategy course, two "cake" electives, and six weeks to go. I had commuted the forty-five minute ride from our one bedroom apartment in Gary to school and back each day so Tony could continue to attend the local Catholic school. He was a straight A student. My GPA was 3.85.

I was leaving my last morning class when I noticed two men in slacks and sport coats standing in the hall. They looked like graduate students, only older. I thought they were waiting to see the professor. With a book bag on my back and a purse slung over my shoulder, I walked toward the snack room. Distracted by my heavy load and the other students rushing in all directions, I was startled by a tap on my shoulder and a voice saying, "Could we speak to you for a minute, Ms. Tangredi?"

I turned and the two men were standing right behind me. "Who are you?"

"If you'll walk down to classroom 110 with us, I can tell you."

"You can tell me now," I responded suspiciously.

"We're with the FBI. I'm Agent Marsh and this is Agent Holt. We can show you our ID here or in room 110."

I looked around and the hall was empty. The kids had disappeared into classes or the snack room.

"Here's good."

They showed me their badges and we walked down the hall to room 110. I was nervous as hell. When we walked into the room, they didn't move to sit down, so neither did I.

The younger looking man, I had him in his late twenties, spoke first. "My name is Joseph Holt and this is Agent Eric Marsh." Holt was 6'1" and thin, and Marsh, who appeared to be in his mid-thirties was 5'8" and looked like a body builder. They were Mutt and Jeff, tall and thin, short and stocky.

"I suppose you're wondering why we want to talk to you," Holt said.

"No, I'm wondering why you are here instead of my apartment. Answer that, then, you can tell me what's going on."

"We've been by your apartment several times and you weren't at home, so we thought we'd try to catch up with you here. We didn't want to stop in at night while your son was home."

That seemed considerate to me. "Okay, what do you want to talk about?" I asked.

"We understand that you are currently in college and you're maintaining yourself with grant money, college loans, and some money from your, shall I call it, part-time work," Holt continued.

"You can call it anything you want. Why are you here?"

"We know you were arrested for solicitation and have a trial pending in a few months. If you are convicted, you could go to jail, lose custody of your son, Anthony, and have a real difficult time finding anyone to employ you after graduation. If you graduate."

"This isn't a federal matter, so I'll ask again Agent Holt, why are you here?"

Holt looked at Marsh and Marsh nodded his head very slightly. Marsh had taken a seat on top of the professor's desk in the front of the room to my left.

Holt responded, "We can make all of that go away."

"Oh, really. Why would you want to do that for little old me, Agent Holt?" My feigned sweetness was evident.

"We'd like you to do a small favor for us."

"And what would that be?" I began to see light at the end of the very dark tunnel.

"Thanks, Joe, I'll take it from here," Marsh said as he turned to speak with me and slid off the desk.

"I'm Eric. May I call you Sandra?" He stuck out his hand.

"Since that's my name, you may." I shook his hand.

"About a year ago we became aware of an organized group of men involved in trafficking underage females from rural areas in the south across state lines for the purpose of prostitution. These are girls as young as fourteen or fifteen, Sandra. Some are brought up here under false pretences such as promises of jobs working in garment factories or waitressing in fancy restaurants; jobs where they could make enough money to help their families. Then they are held against their will and forced into prostitution."

"That's just wrong," I thought. In a flashing moment, I relived the horrible night of my own rape at fifteen. "Why don't you arrest these guys?"

"Arrest we can do, but we need to convict them. For that, we need evidence. We need documentation, witnesses, and testimony.

"You mean the girls won't testify about being held against their will. Isn't that kidnapping?"

"United States Code Title 18, Chapter 77, deals with inter-state trafficking and human slavery. We could also include kidnapping and racketeering, but without evidence, we have nothing. Four months ago, we had two witnesses, girls sixteen and seventeen. We were ready to move in, but the girls disappeared and now we have nothing."

I couldn't believe what I was hearing. I had never heard of anything like this before. "Why didn't you just put them in protective custody?"

"We could have, but we can't protect their families back home and the girls have been told that if they don't do what they're told to do, their families will suffer as well."

"That's extortion isn't it? What do you want from me, Eric?"

"We need someone that's old enough and smart enough to go undercover for us and get the evidence we need to bust these guys."

"Are you asking me to go back to prostitution? You think I could do that?"

"Come on Sandra, we're all grownups here. Have you really been out of it? This is your choice, Sandra. You say "No" and we're out of here. You say, "Yes" then, we can help you. You come highly recommended."

"By whom?"

"Jacqueline Kramer."

"That bitch," I thought, "This is her favor."

"Well, wasn't that nice of Jackie," I smiled.

"Listen Sandra, if you help us with this, we'll make all your problems go away."

"You can make my son's health problems go away?"

"No, we can't do that, but you won't have to worry about any bills. Sandra, this is dangerous work we're asking you to do. We would be willing to pay you as well."

He talked for another five or ten minutes and I asked a few questions about the work. I heard a lot of stuff that would turn your stomach, but in the end, they wanted me to wear a wire and get the goods on everyone from the pimps to the owners and the bosses. They had targeted a hotel in Newport, Tennessee, a town notorious for illegal activity from moonshine to cock fighting and everything in between.

"I need a moment." I walked over to the windows and stared out, my mind racing. Jackie had flipped me for God knows what she got from the Feds. This was my way out, I knew that much. But, what about my little guy, what about school, what about my new life?

I spun around. "I need time to think about your offer, but I can tell you this, if I do this for you, you have to clear all the charges currently pending."

"Done," Marsh, responded.

"I need to finish my last semester."

"You'll have your diploma Sandra."

"You need to pay all Tony's bills, medicine, doctors, and hospitals."

"Considerate it done."

"And you'll pay me four hundred a week."

"That's a little steep. You will be working. How's two hundred sound?"

"Not as good as three hundred."

"Are we negotiating, Sandra?"

"No, that's my price. Think of it this way. You're getting a college grad with over four years of experience for three hundred a week and benefits. How many other candidates do you have with those credentials?"

Marsh smiled. "Okay, here's my card. Just call the office when you've decided."

"One last thing, how long would I be doing this?"

"I don't know Sandra. It depends on what you're able to get for us...six, maybe twelve, months. How long do you think it will take before you make a decision?"

"I need to talk to my son and see about arrangements for his care, and then I'll let you know. You need to put all this in writing, Eric, and you can include an indemnity clause for any prostitution or other charges that may occur while I'm working for you."

Marsh looked at Holt as they walked out. "You did real good, Joe, she's sharp."

After they had gone, I stood there looking out the window. The sun had disappeared behind the clouds. I thought, "Maybe that was an omen of things to come."

Newport, Tennessee

Saturday was Tony's day. Unless he had an activity like Little League or he was going to a friend's house to play, we spent the day together. In the summer, we saw the Cubs play and ate at Cubby Bear Bar on Addison, we went to the Lincoln Park Zoo, or we beached it on Lake Michigan. Tony loved the water. Chicago has a huge park system with over five hundred parks and of course, Lake Michigan. The two of us developed an affinity for the outdoors, which helped when we went to see the Bears play. They don't call it "The Windy City" for nothing. We had a ball! Sundays were for my mom and stepfather. We had dinner together and usually caught a movie or TV show before we headed home.

Tony and I were in Portage Park that Saturday when I approached the subject of my new job.

"Tony, I need to talk to you about something very important. Can we sit on the bench over there?"

"Sure mom." Tony looked a bit nervous.

We went over to one of the benches and sat down. Before I could say anything, Tony burst out, "Mom, if this is about Hillary, I won't do it again, I promise."

"Okay, timeout," I thought. "Well, I'd like to hear your story, Tony."

"I didn't kiss her, she kissed me."

"Hmmm, that's what I thought."My heart was beating faster and I had to keep from smiling. "So, what did Sister say?"

"She said if it happened a third time she was going to have to call you in for a conference."

Now I was stunned. "So, this Hillary kissed you before?"

"No, mom, the first time it was her friend, Marie."

"Ah, Marie. Yes, now I understand." I have to admit that my husband's face flashed in my mind as I looked at Tony. "Well what are we going to do about these girls?" I asked.

"Sister told me that I'm not allowed in the coat closet unless she's with me. I didn't think it was fair, mom. It's not fair. I don't like Hillary and I don't like Marie either."

"Well, I wouldn't worry about it too much. I just wanted to hear your side of the story. You've got a way to go yet before you're going to like girls that much," I offered as I thought we were through and I had covered myself.

"Mom," Tony stared at me like I was an idiot. "I like Sally, Sally Myers!"

I quickly learned my mistake. If I wasn't stunned before, I was stunned now!

"Oh, I see." I gasped out. My mind was racing. I had not prepared for this conversation. "Well, I'm glad we're talking about this."

I had taken a Psychology course in college and I had learned that the two most important things that a parent can do for a child is to build confidence and keep the lines of communication open through trust. So, I asked, "Tony, why haven't we talked about this before?"

His answer was the only one that would not have hurt me. "Mom, you were working so hard with school and your job at night, I didn't want you to worry about me."

"I love you so much," I said and reached for my son; he pulled back.

"How much?" He smiled.

I recovered saying, "A bushel and a peck, and a hug around the neck." It was Tony's favorite and we hugged it out as people walked by and smiled.

"Hey, I have something to tell you."

"What?"

"I got a job!"

"Wow, mom, that's cool! Where? What will you be doing?"

This was the conversation I had prepared for and I had rehearsed a bit. "Well, I have been offered a job working for the FBI."

"The FBI?" Tony's brow wrinkled quizzically.

"It's the Federal Bureau of Investigation."

"Are they like the police?"

"Yes, only for the whole United States. They catch bad guys and put them in jail."

"Mom, are you going to be catching bad guys and putting them in jail? Will you get a gun?" Tony was clearly excited.

"No, honey, I won't have a gun. Let me explain. There are some bad men around here that..."

"You mean the mob guys?" Tony interrupted.

"What?"

"Mom, the mob guys. They're bad guys that live in Chicago, don't you know?"

I was getting a lesson on The Outfit from my eleven-year old son. Swell. "No, honey, this has nothing to do with the Chicago mob guys."

Tony seemed a little less excited.

"These bad guys are from the south. They kidnap young girls and make them work without paying them. The girls are like slaves."

"Why don't they run away or call the police?"

"Remember a couple of years ago when Kevin Lewis was being bullied by that kid named Scott."

"Yes, I hated him." Tony's face tightened. He had no problem showing his emotions.

"Well, that's what it's like for these girls. The bad guys tell them that they'll beat them up if they try to run away. Or worse, they threaten to hurt the girls' families, their mothers or brothers or sisters."

"What would you be doing, mom?" He looked a bit worried.

"I don't know all the job yet honey, but I would be like a spy. They wouldn't even know I was there. Then, when we get enough evidence against the bad guys, we could free the girls and send the bad guys to prison."

"Well, Mom, if it's not in Chicago, where would you be?"

I'd have to move to the south. Right now my job would be in Tennessee."

"Can I go?" Tony asked anxiously.

"I would love for you to go, but I'm not allowed to take you because if they found out I had a child, they might try to hurt you. Do you understand?"

"Yes," he said as he lowered his head.

"Now, should I take this job? Will you be okay?"

Tony thought for a moment, "You have to do it, mom. You have to help those girls."

I hugged my son big time I was so proud of him. "Okay, now here's the deal. I will try to come home every couple of months, but Tennessee is pretty far away. I'll call you every week and you can fill me in on what's happening with Sally Myers."

Tony smiled.

"But you have a big decision to make, so that's why I wanted to talk to you."

"What decision?"

"When I take the job in Tennessee, would you rather live with Grandma and Granddad and go to a new school or would you rather live with Mrs. Lewis and Kevin and stay in Gary. You would still be able to see your grandparents when you want."

"I'll stay with Kevin. That would be cool."

The rest of the day was fun in the park.

On Monday, I contacted Marsh and told him I'd be willing to come on board. We met several times to wrap up details, sign the contract and for him to give me the dope on who, how, when, and where. He also gave me my contact information. I notified the university that I needed a leave of absence, contacted a moving and storage company, and settled-up with my landlord.

I had already asked Mrs. Lewis, the widowed mother of Tony's best friend, if she would be willing to take Tony. I told her I'd pay her one hundred dollars a week for keeping Tony. She was ecstatic. I met with my mother and stepfather to let them know what was going on and to ensure that Mrs. Lewis received her money. We arranged that the rest of the three hundred would go into a bank account I set up. I left my 1968 Pontiac Firebird convertible with Mrs. Lewis, gave my mother a limited power of attorney for any emergency medical needs and the bank account, and then met with Agents Marsh and Holt again to go over the set up.

That week I met Norman Dixon at Brandi's, the bar where I had been freelancing. Norman was anything, but normal. He had a fondness for the unusual. Most of his friends called him Dixie, a nickname I never used, as I never wanted Norman to think of me as his friend. He was about 5'10" and a little over 200 pounds with thinning gray hair. I thought him to be around fifty. I want you to have a good picture of Norman in your mind, so I'll describe his features as best as I can. He was an ugly, disgusting pig.

An FBI undercover agent posing as a John had introduced us. Norman was there for one reason and one reason only; he was recruiting women. He seemed fascinated with my background. The idea of having a former high-price call girl in the stable was irresistible. The fact that half the people in the bar were my former customers increased his interest. I listened carefully as he described the setup in Newport. I told him that I was interested, but that I was interested in getting ahead, too, climbing the ladder, owning a place of my own, eventually. We cut a deal and I told him he could come and get me Monday at 10am. I spent Saturday and Sunday with Tony and my family. My stepfather took me back to my apartment. Leaving Tony was like having my heart ripped out.

******

Monday morning at 9:45, a motorized camper pulled up in front of my apartment. A short, thin man in jeans and a long-sleeved flannel shirt knocked on my door.

"Are you Sandra?"

"I am. Who are you?"

"My name is Roy, "We've come to get you."

I was in jeans, a knit shirt, leather boots, and a leather jacket. I wore no makeup, but I had five hundred dollars in my purse.

"I've got three bags. Can you help me?"

"Sure." He grabbed the big suitcase and my dress bag. I took my makeup bag and purse.

Late April weather in the Chicago area is cool with highs in the low 60's. The sun peaked in and out, as I climbed into the camper. It was clean, but had the smell of stale cigarette smoke. The driver's seat and shotgun seat were both pilot seats with arms. Then, there was a kitchen with a table, stove, fridge, and sink. Several of the seats turned into futons for sleeping and there were shelves for storage above the appliances. In the back were the bathroom and a bedroom.

Roy put my bags into a storage locker and sat in the driver's seat. We pulled out.

Norman sat at the table in a gray suit and sunglasses. "Sandra, come on in and sit down. Let's talk, get to know each other better."

"That's fine with me. Thanks, Norman."

At first, the conversation with Norman was fine. We talked about our destination, The Highland Motor Court in Newport, the hotel Agents Marsh and Holt had told me about. As we finished talking about the business and the players, he became more interested in my history. He asked what I liked and didn't like sexually. He asked question after question and I ducked, dodged, and parried as many as he threw. Finally, he stood up and came around the table. He stood next to me so that his crotch was about six inches from my face. He kept talking as I reached into my bag and pulled out a silver flask I carried and took a drink of vodka.

Newport, Tennessee

"How much to have you open that up and suck and swallow?" He asked pointing at his crotch.

I took another drink of vodka and lit a cigarette, then I turned my head slowly and looked at his crotch; he was stiff. I looked up at his leering, pockmarked, fat face and cooed, "For you Norman, I have a special price."

He smiled.

"Two grand."

"Are you out of your fucking mind?" he screamed. "I can get a blow job for twenty-five dollars!"

"Not from me Norman. Now get that out of my face before your pants catch on fire." I moved the cigarette towards his crotch and Norman backed away.

"You'd better not fuck with me; things could go badly for you." He warned.

"Sit down for a minute Norman and let me explain something to you now."

Norman walked over to the refrigerator and took out a bottle of beer. He took his time so it didn't seem to him that he was doing what I asked, but eventually he sat down.

"I have many friends in Chicago. Do you actually think I'd go to Tennessee with you without knowing the setup and without anyone looking after me? If anything ever happens to me, Norman, I disappear, I'm in an accident, or I break a nail...you're dead...bought and paid for. There is nowhere you could hide from these men, nowhere on this planet.

63

So, I won't fuck with you and you will extend me the same courtesy, understand?"

All the color ran out of his face. Then he managed, "The girls usually want me to take care of them first, if you don't want me to, fine."

"Thank you." I went back to my flask. He rode shotgun. That suited me fine. After we made our first stop for food, Norman took over driving and Roy stayed up front with him. I sat at the table and sipped my vodka, smoked, and played solitaire.

When we got to Newport and pulled up into the Highland Motor Court parking lot, I got out of the camper and was pleased with what I saw. The motel was very nice on the outside, done in a Tutor style. The grounds were well kept and there were lots of cars in the parking lot. The main building was two stories high with a center lobby that had a high ceiling, there were staircases on both sides, and each wing had thirty rooms. Across the parking lot was another free-standing building with two stories and thirty rooms. This building housed the girls in rooms at one end and always on both floors. This ensured that there would never be a working girl in a room over the room of a straight customer.

The lobby was clean with a large fireplace on the back wall that had a fire burning; it took the chill off the night air. The fireplace had a shield of arms that hung on the stonework that ran up to the ceiling. The tan oversize chairs and the dark brown carpet fit the Tutor style perfectly. Across the lobby on the left was an entrance to a restaurant that had both counter service like a diner and tables and booths. It was called The Coffee Shoppe. On the right side of the lobby was a hallway that led to a large conference or ballroom that could hold several hundred people. The fireplace in the center concealed the hotel's kitchen in the rear of the building. A middle-aged woman with blonde hair pulled back in a bun was behind the marble check-in counter.

Before checking into my room, I decided to go to the liquor store. I got a number for a cab service from Alice, the woman with the bun. I told her I was going out for a while and she offered to watch my bags. I used the phone in the lobby. When the cab arrived, I hurried out, settled into the back seat, and told the driver, "Take me to the nearest liquor store."

The cabby looked in the rearview mirror and replied, "Ma'am, this county is dry."

"Then let's go to the next county." I felt myself getting tense. "Dry, what the hell?" I thought.

"The next county is dry, too, ma'am."

"Good God. Then take me to the nearest airport, I'm going home."

"You don't have to do that ma'am," he confided. "There are all sorts of businesses here that sell liquor. A few of the grocery stores and roadhouses do. What do you like to drink?"

"Vodka." I was beginning to feel a bit better.

He turned around in his seat. "I know where to take you. My name's Jake." He extended his hand. I reached out and shook it, and looked at him for the first time. Jake was a good-looking young man in his twenties with a shock of black hair and the cutest grin I'd seen in awhile. He actually had dimples.

"I'm Sandra Love." It was always my opening line. "Tell them your name, honey, that's very important." I could hear Grayson's voice in my head.

We talked as he drove. He asked me if I was a new girl at the hotel. I told him I just got into town. He told me he frequented the hotel on occasion and told me about a couple of the girls he had met. We pulled up in front of a small general store and Jake went in with me.

"Andy, this is Sandra. She works over at The Court."

"I'm pleased to meet you, Sandra." Andy looked like a Teddy Bear and his smile went from ear to ear. He looked me up and down like I was a candy bar. "How can I help you tonight?"

"What kind of vodka do you carry?" I asked.

"Only the best, Smirnoff Red."

That was my introduction to Newport. I smiled, "I'll take a gallon bottle."

Andy looked flustered, "We only sell half-pints."

"No problem, I'll take sixteen."

Jake and I walked out; each of us carried two bags. He drove me back to the hotel, parked in front of the lobby, and turned around. "That will be fifteen dollars."

I gave him twenty.

"Sandra, I really enjoyed meeting you. I was wondering...I mean...I...umm...if you'd want to get together tonight, I could." Jake stammered like a schoolboy, but finally he spit out, "Sandra, I'd like to be your first customer if it's okay with you?"

"It's a little late for that." I thought and smiled. "That would be real nice, Jake."

I checked in with Alice and got my key. Jake helped with the bags. My room was across the parking lot on the second floor, Room 220.

The room was typical for a hotel. On the left was a small round table with two chairs that looked out the picture window. The gold drapes matched those in the lobby as well as the queen size bedspread. The bed was on the left and on the right was an armoire with a TV inside. Two bureaus flanked the armoire. The back of the room had a nice alcove with a sink and vanity mirror that covered the wall and to the left was the door to the bathroom with a tub shower and toilet. I turned the heater on to take the chill off the room, a mistake I corrected a few hours later. Jake looked at me.

I went into Sandra Love mode. "You've been very kind to me Jake, thank you. I can tell we're going to be friends."

Jake started to walk over towards me and I held up my hand. "First, put one hundred dollars on the table, then we can have some fun."

"One hundred dollars, that's a lot, Sandra."

"Tell you what, Jake. When we're through, you can have any part of it back you think was not worth it."

Jake reached into the front pocket of his tight jeans and struggled to pull out his money; his erection seemed to be in the way. He put the money on the table and started taking off his shirt. He pulled it over his head and revealed the hardest abs and nicest chest I'd seen in awhile, not big, but perfectly symmetrical. As I looked at his broad shoulders and well-defined biceps, I thought, "Maybe I should be putting the hundred on the table."

Jake slipped his boots and pants off and stood there in his underwear and socks with that smoking body, a raging erection, and a smile a mile wide.

Now in full Sandra Love mode, I whispered softly, "This is all for you, my Jake."

I slipped off my leather jacket and let it drop to the floor. I unbuttoned my blouse one button at a time. By the time I got to the third button, Jake sat down on the edge of the bed. I slipped off the blouse, turned and reached behind my back and unhooked my bra. When it fell to the floor, Jake hollered, "Yea!"

I reached down and unsnapped my jeans, and then slowly pushed them down to my knees dropping my head as I did and allowing my hair to hang down towards the floor. I swung it back up and stood there in my French cut, white silk bikini panties with my jeans around my knees, saying, "Oh Jake, let me pick these things up first. As I turned to my left bending at the waist and picked up my bra, my breasts hung pendulously beneath me. I stood up, turned my back to Jake, bent over again from the waist, and reached for my jacket. There are only a few men I'd met that would remain seated while I showed them my ass; Jake was not one of them.

"THAT'S ENOUGH!" He shouted as he stood up, grabbed me around the waist, picked me up, and threw me on the bed. I squealed and laughed as he fumbled with my boots and jeans.

"Be gentle." I cooed.

"As soon as I get these damn jeans off you," he almost shouted.

Jake and I had some fine sex. He had what many men don't have, a hard cock, and an easy touch. His body felt wonderful on top of mine and I explored all of it, especially those wide shoulders and that tiny butt. He pulled my hair to arch my back and expose my neck. My neck is my "Go" button. I love being kissed on the neck...kissed, not marked. First in bed, then in the shower, I think I enjoyed soaping down that body more than any other sexual experience I'd had in a very long time. Then Jake picked me up and held me against the wall of the shower as he did me again. I remember thinking, "Newport, Tennessee, this seems like a really nice little town."

Two hours later, I kissed Jake on the cheek and locked the door. The hundred was still on the table. Jake was my first regular. I should have paid him. I turned down the heater and went to sleep. My last thought was about my Tony.

The Outlaw Sandra Love

The Outlaw

The next night I was ready to go to work. Roy had come by my room that afternoon and we had lunch together in The Coffee Shoppe. He reviewed much of what Norman and I had discussed how the girls dressed in short tight skirts, high heels, and showed cleavage, and how they got their customers. I learned that I needed to solicit customers in the restaurant, a situation very different from Chicago where the men came to me. Make no mistake, I was in the tits and ass business, whether it was Chicago or Newport.

Roy showed me the double doors, like saloon doors, in the back of the restaurant that led to a small room that had lava lamps and small strobe lights. When you went in, it was like a movie theater; it took a minute for your eyes to adjust to the darkness. There were six booths in the room, three on either side, and each booth had a tea candle in a red glass holder on the table. The room smelled of incense that eliminated all the food smells of the restaurant. It was as if you stepped into another world; I liked it.

"Bring your customer in here and get the money here, not in the room. If there's a problem, we have people here to take care of you, understand?"

"Yes."

"Then go back through the shop and tell Ted or whoever is on duty that you're 'Going to your room,' it's code."

"Got it."

"You start at 9:15pm. Don't be late as each girl has a different start time. We can't have you all coming in at the same time; you're not the Bears running on to the field." Roy smiled at his joke.

"Not unless you're spelling that B-A-R-E-S," I winked at him.

"Ah...very funny."

All in all, I liked The Court, as everyone referred to the hotel. They did a good deal of business with families and businessmen and our business had no apparent conflict because it was conducted in the back room or in our own room.

I had brought a dozen dresses with me thinking that I would have to take five or six to the dry cleaners at one time and have the others in reserve. One was red, one was white, and ten were black. Most of them were Givenchy. In the sixties, he was the top house thanks to Jackie Kennedy and Audrey Hepburn. Sam had taken me to New York several times and he loved to buy me Gucci; it was an Italian thing. That night I wore a low-cut black evening dress with spaghetti straps. It hung just at the top of my knee, fit well from the waist up, and flowed well when I moved. My expensive black Italian leather heels and clutch bag were pretty standard, but what set the outfit off were the green and gold emerald earrings, necklace, and ring, they had set Sam back thirty-five hundred at Tiffany's. He said they matched my eyes.

When I walked into the restaurant, every head in the room turned, even the girls.

"Hi Sandra," Ted, the greeter and bouncer managed to get out as he stared at my chest.

"Hi Ted, do you have a booth available?"

"You bet, honey!" Ted escorted me to the first booth in the shop. I felt the eyes on me.

I hesitated, "Ted, could I have the one in the back, please?" I pointed to the last booth in the back.

"But Sandra, no one will see..."

"Please."

"Sure, honey." Ted looked confused.

"Thank you." I just smiled and as I walked back, I smiled at everyone whose eyes met mine. I ordered coffee and as I sat in the booth smoking and sipping my vodka laced coffee I thought, "The sisters were right, good manners can take you places money can't."

"Hi, are you Sandra Love?"

I looked up and saw a nice looking young man with tousled blonde hair wearing dark slacks and a white dress shirt that needed pressed. "Yes?"

"I'm Charlie, Charlie Mueller. I'm Jake's friend."

I just looked at him.

"I mean, I'm a friend of Jake's."

"Well, I'm glad to meet you, Charlie. Would you like to join me?"

"Yes ma'am." Charlie scrambled into the booth.

We talked for a while. He told me he also drove a cab, but on day shift. We went into the back room and he told me he'd like everything that Jake and I had done. Aren't men funny? He gave me a hundred dollars and we left the shop. On the way out, I told Ted I was going to my room. Later I learned that the code words did two things: it signaled everything was okay and it gave the pimps a count.

When Charlie and I finished, he told me that there was another young man in the shop at the counter who wanted to see me. By the end of the first week, I had a rather nice group of men who would become regulars. It was my introduction to small town south.

The following week, a man in his thirties came into the restaurant. He looked like a businessman, dressed in a dark blue suit, matching tie with a yellow stripe, and a white shirt. He wore glasses and he looked very familiar. He came back to my booth and we quickly went into the back room. He leaned forward and whispered, "Sandra, it's me, Eric Marsh."

"As if," I thought, but I played along. "Wow, a pair of glasses, that's a hell of a disguise." That made him smile. "We can't talk here; let's go to my room," We went up to the room and he gave me a new contact phone number.

"Try to call this number on a regular basis. You can keep it in your purse until you commit it to memory. If someone finds the number, it won't get you in trouble. A little old lady answers and anyone calling will think they've reached a private residence. She's everyone's grandmother. Why haven't you called?"

"I need a place where I can call privately. I'm not calling you from this room phone. Right now I'm more interested in fitting in here; most of the women rarely leave," I told him.

"Okay, I'm sure you'll figure that out. Meanwhile, your job is to get information on the pimps and the bosses. I brought you this." He took off his jacket, tie, and shirt, and he was wearing a wire.

"Listen to me, Eric, because I don't intend to die here. It is much too early to be wearing a wire. I haven't even met the boss yet." I was sitting on the bed and he was leaning against the table. I stood up, unzipped the back of my dress, and let it fall to the floor. His mouth dropped a bit. "And where exactly would you like me to hide it?"

Eric stood up and matching my sarcasm said, "Bend over and I'll show you."

I laughed out loud. Eric smiled.

"Listen, I know you're a tough girl, just don't underestimate these guys. I don't want that on my conscience."

I could feel myself going into Sandra Love mode. Eric Marsh with his shirt off was very attractive. "That's so nice of you, Agent Marsh," I walked over to him in my panties and heels, put my arms around his neck and pressed my breasts into his chest, "You care about me, don't you?"

Eric reached up and removed my hands, "Yes, I do. Now, put your dress back on, Sandra."

"I will, if you put your shirt back on." We both dressed. I turned to him and said, "When I'm ready for the wire, I'll let you know."

"Okay, just be sure we hear from you once a week or we'll have to send someone in."

"Got it, thanks. Now leave a hundred on the table and skedaddle."

"A hundred dollars?"

"They have a count system here, when you came up you became a John; just put it on your expense report."

He put four twenties, a ten and two fives on the table.

"Good night, Agent Marsh." I cooed.

He waved his hand at me and left.

******

During the first week, Norman was a regular visitor to my booth. He always wanted sex, but I refused. Finally, I told him, "Norman, I'm not interested in sex with you. If we have any relationship, it will be strictly business."

Norman didn't get angry. He told me if I didn't want to go to bed with him that was fine. At the end of the week, Norman phoned my room around three in the afternoon and asked me to come to The Coffee Shoppe. When I got there, there was a sign on the door that read, "Closed for cleaning." I tried the door and it was open. I went in and saw Norman sitting at a table in the back with Roy and Ted. One other man sat at the counter drinking coffee. I walked back to the big round table.

"Go upstairs and get our money," Norman said.

"Where's our money?" I replied.

"Haven't you been putting our money in the dresser in your room?"

"There's money in there."

"Go get our money."

"If I get the money, what are we going to do with it?" I asked him.

"That's my money."

"What do you mean your money?"

"You see, you're working for me here. That's my money, so go to your room and get it."

"Okay, I'll be right back."

I went to my room, counted the money, and discovered there was twelve hundred dollars. I made a lot more money in a week's time in Chicago, but of course, I spent a lot more money too.

When I got back to the restaurant, I handed Norman the fat envelope. He opened it and out fell the money in little confetti-size pieces. He stared at the shredded money on the table; his face first turned white, then red, and finally purple. "You fucking bitch," he shouted. "You tore up my money! You work for me and you tore up my fucking money!"

"I don't work for you Norman, get that straight right now," I stated calmly. "When I came down here the deal was I work for the house. I don't have a pimp and I don't know what you mean 'I work for you,' but I know this, if I sell my ass, I get the money; if you sell your ass, you get the money."

Roy and Ted almost fell on the floor laughing. Norman was speechless. The man at the counter came over and pulled out one of the chairs, "Would you like to sit down, Sandra?" I hesitated. "Please, it's alright," he said. I sat down and he sat next to me.

I lit a cigarette, "Are you the owner of this establishment?" I asked.

"Yes."

"My name is Sandra Love. What's yours?"

"My name is James Martin McLeod, but most people call me Codlock."

I later learned that Codlock is a mountain term for someone who only bets on a sure thing. He'd earned the name because of his past gambling success; Codlock was a poker player. He was in his mid-fifties, six feet tall, of heavy build, and had a salt and pepper beard he kept neatly. Roy and Ted were still laughing.

"What are you guys laughing about?" Codlock asked.

They stopped laughing. When he didn't get an answer, he looked at Norman. "Is there a problem here, Dixie?"

"That damn bitch tore up my money."

Codlock looked at me. "Sandra?"

"Look, I was invited down here. These guys asked me to come. I don't know what this go round is about having an old man. I work for myself with a house split. You just said you own this place, didn't you?"

"Yes."

"Then I work with you. I keep my money and you get room rent for each customer. If you agree, we're in business. If you don't agree, I go to the airport and go home."

"Sandra, I want you to stay. I don't think we were prepared for someone with your background, but we want you to stay. You're good with customers and I think after you've been here awhile you'll be good for our business." He looked at Norman and said, "All of our businesses, wouldn't you agree, Dixie?"

"Yea, she's good." He mumbled.

"Usually the girls here have a pimp, but it's okay with me if you work alone as long as you pay rent for each customer. I usually get twenty- five percent."

"Not on what I charge; how's fifteen sound?"

"Not as good as twenty," Codlock responded with a smile.

"Deal." We shook hands.

"I also charge four hundred a month for the room."

"How's one hundred sound?" I asked.

"Not as good as three hundred." Codlock smiled again.

"Okay then, two hundred it is. Do we have a deal?" I extended my hand again.

His smile got bigger. "Yes, I like you Sandra; you've got spunk." We shook hands.

Then Codlock added, "By the way Sandra, how much money was that?"

"Twelve hundred." I told him.

"You owe me two-forty." Codlock was quick with numbers.

"How about I give you one-twenty and he gives you one-twenty?" I pointed at Norman.

Codlock laughed out loud, "Yeah, that's good. We were definitely not ready for you."

"Thanks; one more thing," I smiled. "If I pull my shifts, I come and go as I please. I need time to shop, go to a salon, get my clothes dry-cleaned, and eat out occasionally. If I don't have a pimp, and all the rules that go with them, there is no reason why I have to stay on the premises all the time. I need to get out some."

Roy and Norman were both scowling. I could tell they did not like where this conversation was going.

They really looked disgruntled when Codlock agreed, "That's good."

"Thank you. That'll make life more livable."

Finally able to get away from the motel, I had a chance to learn about the town of Newport. It's in the eastern Blue Ridge Mountains of Tennessee. It's also in Cocke County, which I thought was really funny. At the time, it had a population of around twenty-five thousand. The history of the area included moonshining, prostitution, and cockfighting. In the sixties and seventies, marijuana growing was also on the rise.

The Outlaw

I learned that most men carried pistols, mainly Smith and Wesson 38's, tucked in the waist of their pants and hidden by a shirt or jacket. Every week there was at least one killing or a shooting in the area, most associated with drugs and alcohol.

I was very careful when I went out. I made my calls from a pay phone in the general store. My first call to Mrs. Lewis' house lasted an hour. Tony and I talked and he filled me in on everything he was doing at school and with the Lewis family. I told him how much I loved and missed him and he told me he missed me, too. When I spoke with my mom, she told me that he was doing fine, except he had a seizure while he was riding a bike and took a spill that required stitches. I cried.

I called Tony every week and checked in with Marsh when I could. Every once in a while, I spotted one of the local pimps parked outside the store. The men were watching me because I didn't have a pimp. None of them profited from my work and I had freedoms their women didn't, but after awhile, the men quit following me. Business was good and they figured I wasn't worth the trouble.

I earned the title of outlaw, a prostitute without a pimp.

The Outlaw Sandra Love

New Friends

Some afternoons before I went to work, I would sit in
The Coffee Shoppe and chill. I like time to myself,
time to reflect. It was a nice sunny day in October. I
was thinking about my summer trips back to see Tony
for Memorial Day, July 4th, and Labor Day weekends.
I had stayed four or five days each trip and we had
some amazing times. Tony turned eleven in
September and we celebrated his birthday while I was
home for Labor Day. Just two more years and my son
would be a teenager. I thought about my teenage
years and all my mistakes; you know how your mind
flits from one thing to another when you're
daydreaming with time. I reached down, pulled my
flask out of my purse, and poured some into my
coffee, it went well with my honey bun. I'd been there
about twenty minutes when a tall, good-looking man
walked up to my table.

"May I sit down?" He asked.

"Sure," I said, "help yourself."

"I'm Freddy LeBlanc, he said as he lit a cigarette and
ordered a coffee from the waitress who was waiting
my booth.

"You need anything, Sandra?" She asked.

"I'm good Vanessa, thanks."

His appearance surprised me. He looked to be in his
late thirties and was very handsome, tall, and slim
with a nice head of dark hair. He wore a custom-

tailored, double-breasted silk suit with a silk shirt and conservative striped tie, unusual for the seventies. His cologne was the kind that makes your mouth water. Then I spotted the GP watch. I recognized it as Sam had worn a Girard Perregaux HF Chronometer that he bought in New York.

"So, you're name is Sandra," he confirmed. "Where are you from?"

"Chicago," I replied.

"How did you get to this small hick town?"

"I might ask you the same thing. You look too well-dressed to be from here."

"I'm trying to open up a business over near Knoxville."

"Well, some friends asked me to come down here and work awhile. I needed a change of scenery so I decided to come."

As we kept talking, I grew more impressed with Freddy. I certainly hadn't seen anyone at the Highland Motor Court as handsome, well-dressed, and articulate. I complimented him on his suit and commented on the watch. Then I asked him the question that every single woman asks a man when they first meet.

"What do you do for a living?"

"I'm in the entertainment industry."

"You make movies?"

He smiled, "Nothing that elaborate."

"Down here, when you're dressed as well as you are, some people might take you for a pimp." I prodded him a bit.

"If I was, how would you feel about that?"

I realized he was toying with me. "Fine, but I have no need for a pimp."

"Not even a good one?" He smiled.

"Freddy, if you're done jousting?"

He raised his eyebrows, surprised by my confronting him.

"You know who I am?" I asked.

"Yes, Sandra Love, I heard about you."

"You seem like a really nice guy, Freddy, but I already have an agreement for my stay here. No pimp."

"Then we can just be friends," he said. "How about going to dinner sometime when you're off work?"

"Yeah," I thought for a minute. "I'd like to get out for awhile."

"I'm off tomorrow night." I told him.

So, the next night, Freddy and I had dinner. We had a great time together and he filled me in on his background. Freddy got into crime as a teenager, breaking into places and stealing anything he could sell. Later, he turned to armed robbery, hitting small stores before he tried bars and then banks. He eventually decided to invest some of his money. Freddy and a friend named Jack bought a truck stop in Florida; that's when he got into prostitution. He had been in business for about three years when he decided to come to Tennessee. He told me how he hated the heat. He sold his share to Jack and came north. Right after he left, the police raided the place and closed it down. He left with a stash of cash and Jack went to jail. Freddy was a lucky guy. As we became friends, we started seeing each other on a regular basis; most of the time we went shopping together in Knoxville.

On one of our shopping trips to Knoxville, I called my mom to check on her plans for Thanksgiving. She told me she was taking Tony on a trip to Wisconsin to see some relatives. I talked to Tony and told him that I would be home for Christmas vacation. He wanted an update on the bad guys and asked did I get any of them yet. He was so cute.

My conversation with Tony was a reminder for me of why I was there. I needed evidence and I couldn't get it unless I became closer to the other girls. I used the holiday to organize a Thanksgiving dinner for the girls, the pimps, and Codlock. When I took the idea to the boss man, he liked it right away and asked if I would coordinate it with the staff. Norman and Roy seemed neutral as they had planned a trip to Florida for that week, but Freddy and the others were very supportive. It reminded me of some of the events I used to help with at Tony's school. I met with the girls and asked them if they had a favorite dish that they had at Thanksgiving when they were growing up. Some did and got excited over the meal. I worked it out with Woody, our cook, to let them help prepare their dishes. The girls really got into it and even helped me with serving so that Vanessa, Woody, Ted, Alice, and Codlock could sit and eat with us. Everyone had a blast, even the three customers that we had; one of them was my Jake. It was my first step in getting close to the girls. They all had a great time.

A week later, I was in The Coffee Shoppe and it was full of men and women, eating, drinking, smoking, and talking. It was around ten-thirty in the evening and near the end of my shift, as I had pulled an early shift that night. Suddenly, I got a strong whiff of the great outdoors. I looked up and a huge, burly-headed man with brown hair and a bushy beard stood alongside my table. Dressed in dirty jeans, an old flannel shirt, a hunting coat, and a cowboy hat, he looked down at me with his dark eyes, shark eyes.

I looked him up and down and thought, "Now that's a mountain of a man."

"Mind if I sit with you awhile?" He asked.

"No, not at all. Have a seat," I muttered.

"My name is Robert Allen McIntyre. Most people call me Robert Allen. What's your name?"

"Sandra. I work here. In fact, I'm on duty now."

"I know. I'm not here for sex," he said, "Will you go out and have coffee with me when your shift is over?"

"Well, I'm real pleased to meet you Robert Allen, but I'm having coffee here. So why would I go out with you for coffee?" There was something about this big, burly man that made me nervous. He looked like the Brawny Man, but he wasn't selling paper towels; that was for sure.

He motioned for me to lean closer as he leaned across the table, "Because then we can talk privately. Agent Marsh thought that might be a good idea."

A half hour later, I met him in the parking lot and got into his truck. We drove around the streets of the small Tennessee town. He parked down by the Pigeon River.

"So who are you, Robert Allen?"

"I guess you'd say I'm an entrepreneur."

"Well, aren't we all?" I paused.

"I work in a wide variety of fields, from moon shining to weed farming. If it involves making money, I'll do it, but my primary job is solving problems."

"That sounds a bit ominous, Robert Allen."

"It is what it is, Sandra."

"Why are you working for the feds?"

"Same as you, I got my tit in a ringer last year; it's this or prison. All you really need to know is, Marsh does not want anything to happen to you. It's my understanding that if something happens to you some very bad things could happen to people here. Guess you've got friends in high places, Sandra."

"I have many friends, thank you."

"So you know, we've got to be careful, Sandra," he warned. "This is a very dangerous game. Believe me, there is an organization down here. It may not be on the same scale as Chicago, but it is just as deadly. You screw up; your ass is gone. Understand?"

"Yes."

"Good, do you own a gun?"

"No," I told him.

"Do you know how to shoot a pistol?"

"My ex-husband took me shooting once."

"I have a .25 semi-automatic back at my place. I'll give it to you and give you some pointers. I'm sure you can find a way to keep it hidden."

Several days later, Robert Allen drove me into the mountains and parked the car in a field. He loaded the semi-automatic with six bullets. "Don't ever add the seventh," he cautioned. "The gun might jam."

He got dozens of empty drink bottles out of the car and set up ten in a row. Robert Allen taught me many things about shooting a gun: range and accuracy, how to load and hold the gun, how to sight the gun, stance, breathing, and trigger pull. He also taught me the mechanics of the gun including how to clean it and the difference between semi-automatic pistols with a clip and one chamber and revolvers with multiple chambers, but the most important thing he taught me was, "The first shot is the most important thing about firing a gun to kill. If you do this part right, everything else is no worries. If you don't, it gets a lot more complicated."

Robert Allen and I went shooting a dozen or more times until I was very good with a gun. We used paper targets that he stapled to trees; they were in the shape of a human body. He'd have me walk through a path where he had stapled the targets to trees on both sides. Then, he would walk behind me. Suddenly, he would shout left or right and I'd have to turn and shoot at the target. He loved the game. I became pretty confident about my shooting ability, but still didn't like having a gun. Then he taught me one last lesson.

"Sandra, never point a gun at someone and not shoot it. If you feel the need to point the gun, you need to fire it, understand?"

"I do, thank you Robert Allen."

On the way back down the mountain, we stopped at an overlook. We got out of the car and he showed me the view, and it was beautiful. A rock wall about three feet high separated us from a three hundred foot deep ravine.

"There's many a body that's been dropped down there," he remarked rather casually. I said nothing. I thought to myself, "That's way more than I need to know."

Robert Allen was a different character altogether. He was soft spoken and good hearted and would help anybody. He owned a car repair garage. He would fix old people's trucks and cars and not charge them anything, but I think it was a front, for most of the money he made was from criminal activity. He was well known and well liked. Robert Allen had a slow fuse, but he had a violent temper and when it went off, there was hell to pay. Bull-headed and focused, God help you if he was pissed at you. It was like that movie "Jaws"; he just kept coming. He was thirty-eight when I met him. He had been a marine after high school and had served in Korea before coming home. When I was with him, he made me feel different than when I was with any other man, he made me feel safe. I liked that and I liked Robert Allen very much.

New Friends

On Friday, December 24th, Christmas Eve morning, I woke to someone knocking on my motel room door. I raised my head and looked at the clock. It was a little after 8am. I wondered who it could be. I knew it wasn't a customer because I was off. I was leaving that evening for a week to see Tony and my folks for the holidays.

I threw off the cover, rolled out of bed, and stumbled to the door bare ass naked. I had entertained a customer until 2am the night before and was hung over. I opened the door just enough to see who was there. A blast of cold air hit me in the face. It was Robert Allen.

"What are you doing here? You know I like to sleep in on my days off!"

"Hey, it's Christmas and I brought you some presents. You're going home today aren't you?"

Immediately I felt bad. I told him to come on in. "You'll have to excuse me. I'm usually grouchy when I first get up. Sit down while I get some clothes on."

I went back to get my robe from the hanger, but before I put it on, I turned around and Robert Allen was staring at me-no that's wrong...he was sort of transfixed, staring at me naked. Then I noticed that he was dressed better than usual, wearing new jeans and a new red plaid flannel shirt. His beard was well trimmed and he wasn't wearing his hat. His full head of dark brown hair was clean and shiny. He had a burlap bag in his right hand.

"Well, aren't we looking good today," I said. "I believe you have on new clothes."

Nothing. He was still staring.

I smiled.

His eyes were on my body, but slowly they rose until our eyes met. Then I saw something I hadn't seen since I was a child. I saw the look in Robert Allen's eyes, the same look that my dad used to have for my mother. I know we stood there for a minute; he just kept on looking at me.

"Robert Allen!" I broke the silence.

"Y-you're very beautiful." He said softly.

It would take me a long, long time to figure out how difficult that was for him to say.

"Thank you, Robert Allen," I responded.

He dropped the bag on the floor and started to walk towards me, very slowly. It's hard for me to share, let alone explain the feeling.- excitement, nervousness, breathlessness. His hands touched my shoulders; they were so big! He slid his hands down my arms and then under my arms to my back. I felt like the leaf before the storm as my robe fell to the floor. Robert Allen always smelled like the outdoors. The smell was so natural, so wholesome, and so sexual; I always got a little horny in the woods. I thought of it as a natural thing. He picked me up as if I was nothing and laid me down on the bed. He lay on top of me. I felt his mass, but not his weight, and then his mouth covered mine and I felt his tongue in my mouth. He kissed me forever. I was not use to foreplay. I was more than ready to go, but instead his huge hands kept gently exploring my body. I kept thinking, "Please, now."

In my whole life, I have never experienced anything close to that morning when Robert Allen made love to me. Maybe it was the hangover, maybe it was Robert

New Friends

Allen, or maybe it was the first time I actually felt true love. Whatever it was, it was fantastic. I will remember it until I die.

"My folks gave me these for Christmas," he smiled as I watched him put his clothes back on. "Now come over here and open your presents. I've got other gifts to deliver today."

That's when I remembered I'd given him money to buy toys, clothes, and food for poor kids in his community of Jones Cove.

"Have you delivered the presents for the children?" I asked.

"Yeah, I gave those things to their folks yesterday. I wanted the children to think Santa Claus brought them. Their parents know where they came from, Sandra."

"Now I'm ready to see what you have in that bag," I said. "It must be alive because it's moving."

Robert Allen opened the bag and out jumped a black kitten with big green eyes. It looked at me and immediately ran under the bed.

Then he pulled out a bag of cat food, a kitty litter box, and two bowls for the cat, one for food, and one for water. I was both shocked and pleased.

"You took my wanting a cat seriously," I said. Where did you find the kitten?"

"Oh, his mother just took up at my folk's house and she had the kittens a couple of months ago. He's half wild; you may have a time taming him."

I gave Robert Allen a hug.

"Thanks. It was very thoughtful of you to think of me, but who's going to take care of him while I'm gone."

"I'll do it, that's why I brought the food and the litter box. I'll need your key."

"How about you drive me to the airport and I'll give it to you then."

"Suits me, but you're not leaving until this afternoon. What do we do until then?"

"Well, you could play with the pussy," I cooed.

We fed the kitten and played with him. Robert Allen had also brought some catnip shaped like a mouse, some shoelaces, and a flashlight. I asked him what the flashlight was for and he said, "Watch this."

He flashed the light on the floor and moved the spotlight around until the kitten spotted it. He was very still as he watched the light moving slowly across the floor. Then he pounced. Robert Allen moved the light and the kitten chased it around with its paws while I laughed my ass off. Finally, in tears, I pleaded, "Don't tease him anymore." I picked him up and put him on the bed; he curled up beside me.

"We need a name for him," I told Robert Allen. It was several hours before I decided on a name. I named him after a friend of Robert Allen's who was a hit man and a dope dealer. He was a bad dude, but he and Robert Allen were friends going back to elementary school. He was quiet and very loyal to Robert Allen. He had dark black hair, just like my cat. So, I named the cat Jerry Crosby Miller. Jerry died several years later in a hail of gunfire and he never forgave me for naming my cat after him.

Home for the Holidays

"Mom!"

If there is any word in the English language that evokes more meaning and love when shouted, I have not yet heard it.

Tony ran across the thirty feet of floor from where people were waiting for passengers to the entrance where passengers enter the airport. I dropped my luggage and present bags and we hugged it out big time. It seemed everyone around us was doing the exact same thing. I was surrounded by tears, laughter, and love, as my mom and stepfather joined the dozens of others greeting their families and friends at Christmas.

"Brrrr..." I shivered as we approached the outside door.

"Sandra, all you have is that leather jacket?" My mom asked.

I was wearing the same outfit I wore when I left eight months before." It doesn't get that cold in Tennessee mom. I have a sweater I brought in my bag, but it's heavy and I couldn't get it on under this jacket. I'll be fine.

Tony held me close. He was nearly my height, all 5' 3" of me. My stepfather pulled up in the car, got out, and opened up the trunk, I caught him winking at my mom and Tony who stood behind me not helping with the bags. Then my stepfather pulled my mink out of the trunk and smiled.

"Joe!" I squealed and hugged him as he struggled to put the coat on me.

"It's going down to ten tonight," he whispered in my ear, "thought you might need this."

"Thanks...thanks for everything." I hugged him tight.

We got in the car and Tony and I talked in the backseat while my stepfather drove. I felt like a queen. We ate out and exchanged gifts at midnight. Everyone slept in on Christmas Day; around 9am, I smelled coffee and stuck my head out of the quilt. I was sleeping on the couch with the quilt as cover.

"Black and two sugars, right?"

My mom had a tray with two steaming coffee mugs, cream, and the sugar bowl. I love the smell of a hot cup of coffee. I wrapped myself in the quilt. I normally sleep naked; never could go to sleep with clothes on, but I was wearing my panties and a Chicago Bears football shirt, #40.

"I could use a hand in the kitchen, today."

"Oh, mom, of course;" I looked at my mom's face, not engaged. "I know that look, what's wrong?"

"Just worried...I guess you never stop worrying about your children."

"Mom, I know it's dangerous, but I have good people, let me rephrase that, I have friends looking after me. I'll be alright."

"I know, Sandra, it's not you I'm worried about."

"Who, then? Tony? You told me the doctor said he was getting better. What aren't you telling me, mother."

"I'm not, not telling you anything. I'm here to tell you something and you need to listen to me very carefully, Sandra."

I felt the panic that I always felt when I thought Tony was in trouble subside a bit. My response was softer and no longer accusatory. "What mom, what is it?"

Mom sipped her coffee, the pregnant pause. "Have you given any thought to what you'd tell your son if he found out what you are doing in Tennessee?"

I snapped, "Make no mistake, mother, I would kill the person who told him." I could tell my response angered my mother. She responded quickly.

"That's no answer!" She snapped back. "He's going to have questions as time goes by. You have to be prepared to answer them. You can't lie to him; if he ever finds out, you could lose him."

Her response scared me, "I don't know how I'd live without him. I need to get out of this shit-storm I'm in. When he's older, I'll tell him, if he asks. I'll know when he's ready."

"Listen Sandra, I don't know who's behind this, but Mrs. Lewis has told me that Tony has been taking some guff at school over rumors about what you're doing. Could Paul..."

"Paul Fulcher?"

"Yes."

"Why would you think Paul would..."

"Mrs. Lewis said she runs into him occasionally and he always asks about you."

"I don't know. Paul wouldn't. I don't have the time to..." My brain was running a thousand miles an hour.

"You need to touch base with Tony while you're home, reassure him."

"Okay, mom, I'm on it. I need some time to think about it. Thanks for the heads up. Let's enjoy our Christmas. Do you have any vodka?"

It was a good Christmas. After listening to my stepfather bitch for a few hours about how the turkey smell was making him drool, we sat down at the table at noon. We did the whole turkey meal thing; it was outstanding! After the meal was over, I talked to my family.

"There are a few things I'd like to tell all of you." The room was very quiet.

"First, I love all of you very much. Nothing will ever change that."

"I love you too, mom." Tony reassured me as he reached for my hand.

"Me, too, Sandra, I love you!" Joe echoed.

I looked at my mom; she blew me a kiss and her mouth formed a silent, "Love you," as her eyes moistened.

"I have made some mistakes in my life and I am sorry. The job I am doing now is dangerous, but I am working with some very good people and I don't want you to worry about me, I'll be fine. I miss you all and I can't wait until the job I'm doing is over. I just don't know right now how long it will be, but I want you to know, when it's over I will come home and we will be a family together again."

I pushed back from the table and ran into my old bedroom, where Tony had slept, and fell on the bed crying into the pillow so no one would hear. I thought I was having a nervous breakdown. Too much vodka! I cried and cried until I felt a hand rubbing my back, softly. I turned over. Tony sat on the edge of the bed; my parents stood behind him.

"It's okay, mom, it's okay."

I sat up and we hugged. God it felt so good to hold my son. Finally, I composed myself and pushed away so I could get a good look at him. Tony smiled, "Ya got boogers mom." He grabbed my arm and lifted it until Gayle Sayers' sleeve wiped the snot off my lip. I laughed; we all laughed.

We spent the next few days together as a family. We did the Christmas tree in the plaza, skating on the lake; we saw a James Bond movie and we shopped. Boy, did we shop. I even got a gift for Robert Allen, a new Buck knife. I thought about him a lot. "Lord, am I in love?"

We had our lunches out. Each day I strutted around in the gift my family gave to me, my new Eddie Bauer down parka. The hooded, hip length jacket was warm as toast. Now here is a surprise; it was green! On the last day, we all went to the airport together and caught lunch. Joe looked tired, but he managed a smile when I told them about my cat, Jerry Crosby Miller.

We said our goodbyes. I told Tony, "Be strong."

He had some advice for me, "You too, mom."

******

When I got back from Chicago, I called Robert Allen to pick me up. There was no answer. I called Freddy and he picked me up and took me back to The Court. He had stayed in town for the holidays, he and Codlock seemed to be hitting it off pretty well. Freddy had brought in four girls he had worked with before and was now pimping for them at The Court. I went up to my room and he went to the restaurant. I opened the door to my room with a key I got at the front desk and Jerry Crosby Miller greeted me. I picked him up and held him inside my parka for a few minutes, petting and kissing him; he purred. Then I gave him some food and fresh water and changed out his box. I showered up and when I opened the shower curtain, Jerry was lying on the top of the toilet tank. I toweled off, and went out and sat in front of the mirror. He followed me out and rubbed up against my legs as I sat on the stool. I picked him up and placed him on the vanity and he sat there and watched as I put my makeup on.

Someone knocked on my door. Jerry jumped up and went into the bathroom.

Norman and Roy were still in Florida, but three of their girls were knocking on my door, I opened it a bit. It was The L Sisters, Linda, Lola, and Lilly. The L Sisters was the nickname these three girls chose because their working names all started with the letter L. They were as much sisters as their names were their real names, but they were close.

"Sandra, can we come in?"

"Sure." I opened the door and the girls came in. They wanted to find out about my Christmas. I was a bit evasive just telling them I spent time with family and friends, and showed off my new jacket. When I asked them about their holiday, it got quiet. Suddenly, it dawned on me that Christmas could be the happiest time of the year for some and the saddest time for others, especially young girls. I was filled with new motivation from my visit home. This was my opportunity to bond with these girls. I needed to get close to them in order to get the evidence I needed.

"You guys seem a bit down; holidays can be like that. How would you all feel about a New Year's Eve party?"

Linda responded, "But it's Tuesday and Friday is New Years Eve, how could we..."

"Stop right there Linda. Just tell me if you want to celebrate the New Year and I'll do the rest, but remember this, you all will be working."

"That's fine with me; I'm up for a party!" Lola said.

"Count me in." Lilly chimed in.

"What do we do, Sandra?" Linda asked.

"I have to get Codlock behind this. If it puts money into his pocket, he'll go along for sure. Let me talk to him. Freddy's with him in the restaurant. You guys stay here with Jerry Crosby Miller while I go talk to him."

"Miller, the hit man...where is he?" Linda asked looking around nervously.

"Wait here a second." I smiled and went into the bathroom and got my cat off the back of the toilet. "Not him. This is my cat. I named him Jerry Crosby Miller because they both have black hair."

"Oh, he's so cute." The girls were still fawning over Jerry as I dressed and left the room.

I went downstairs and across the lot to the restaurant. Ted was on duty greeting and seating.

"Hi Sandra, how was your Christmas?

"Very nice, Ted thanks. Santa brought me this new coat. How was yours?"

"Eddie Bauer, they're nice. I spent all my money on wine, women, and song," Ted responded.

"Well, go easy on the wine and the song, they're killers." Ted laughed. I spotted Freddy in my booth waving for me to come over. Codlock was with him. I walked over and slid in next to Freddy.

"Hey, Sandra, good holiday?" Codlock asked as he ate his dinner.

"Absolutely. How was yours?"

"It was boring, not much action. Everyone's at home with their families on the holidays; I lost revenue and things are tight."

"Well, you have New Year's Eve coming up. Guess you've got something big planned."

"Actually, that's what Freddy and I were just talking about."

"Really?"

"Yea, he suggested that we ought to have some special party or something. I thought you might like to help."

"Whoa, there, Mr. Codlock. This isn't Thanksgiving dinner for the staff you're talking about. You do realize you only have three days to put something together."

"What do you think, Sandra?" He asked.

"Well, you need some sort of package deal."

Freddy smiled, "Told ya."

"Can I make money on that?"

"Sure, some margin on the package and then liquor and the girls. Just one thing, they can't bring in their own liquor. You sell the bottles under the table."

Codlock's eyes narrowed as he thought it through.

"You've got three days to advertise and promote, order, and prepare food, and get the girls and the liquor lined up. Are Norman and Roy back, yet?"

"No."

"Well..." Codlock interrupted me.

"Sandra, if I gave you full reign, could you pull this off in three days?"

I held my hands up signaling 'time out.' In my mind I thought, "How many times does something like this drop in your lap...just take it slow." I knew I could do it in two days. I summoned up my most concerned look and responded, "Look, this is going to be tough, but if you give me full reign I'll do it."

Codlock's face lit up like a pumpkin at Halloween, "Thanks, Sandra, I..."

"I need some things." I interrupted him.

"What? Tell me."

"Him!" I pointed at Freddy.

"I'm in," Freddy agreed.

"You got him," Codlock confirmed.

"I'll handle the girls and everything else. It won't cost you a thing, but sometime I may ask you to do me a favor."

"I understand how it works." Codlock said.

"I'll be back in an hour. I'll meet you two in your office. Freddy, you start working on a package: room, menu, hors d'oeuvres, surf and turf, free Champaign at midnight, and continental breakfast. Price it out...don't forget a DJ."

The L Sisters were excited and I told them to get the others ready, as it would be a heavy night. They were all to dress to the teeth. I got my Jake to do the advertising; between him and Charlie Mueller I think every guy and gal in Newport interested in going out on New Year's Eve was headed to The Court either alone or with a date. Codlock made a little over fifteen thousand in one night and business picked up in the New Year. Ted's count was the highest single night ever, but most importantly, it was another opportunity to talk and work with all the girls. They were real appreciative. I think it had been a long time since anyone had done anything for them and it felt like we were coming together as a group. Saturday afternoon, when I walked into the restaurant for lunch, I saw Codlock seated at the counter. He looked up and saw me, grabbed his coffee and newspaper, and headed to my booth.

"That was something pretty special last night; you did real good."

"Thanks, I had fun."

"Everyone did. You made a name for yourself last night. There were some big-wigs here; they asked about you."

"Really?"

"Really. I'm working on something big, Sandra. We have backing and I'm putting together a team. I think you could help us launch this."

"Well, it sounds interesting. What is it?"

"I've got to run now; we'll talk more, later. Thanks again, Sandra, I won't forget."

When Norman and Roy got back from Florida late Sunday night, they had two new girls with them, young girls.

I still had not heard from Robert Allen.

Monday morning I got up early, showered, dressed, and walked to the lobby. I told Alice I was going for a walk to test out my new parka. She smiled and I think she knew how proud I was to be wearing it. It took about twenty minutes to walk downtown from the hotel; it was windy and cold.

 I went to the store where I usually called from and dialed.

"Hello."

"Hi, Emma, this is Sandra, ID 05151940, is Eric there?"

The older woman on the other end of the phone played her part perfectly." Hi Sandra, I think he's in his room, just hold a minute."

I waited.

"Hello."

"Eric, it's Sandra."

"What's up?"

I learned a long time ago in Chicago, never talk on the phone, and if you have to talk on the phone, never say anything incriminating, "I just wanted you to know I had a nice holiday vacation. By the way, those two friends of mine who went south for the holidays got back last night and they brought two of their kids back with them. So I was thinking that maybe we could all get together soon."

"Well, that's good news. We'll try and set something up."

"What about that problem we had the last time I saw you."

"Oh, we're working on that. We can make that go away with a little planning depending on where we get together."

"Good, I'll call you next week. While I got you, that friend of ours, I haven't heard from him since before Christmas."

"He's visiting family," Eric interjected, "I saw him while you were away. He seems different; is everything okay at your end?"

"I'll say." I think Eric could hear me smiling through the phone. I hung up. Robert Allen was okay, "Excellent."

The Outlaw Sandra Love

The Santee Plan

A few days later, Freddy and I took a ride through the country in his white 1970 Lincoln Continental. The sun was shining and the air was crisp, but not cold, just a beautiful day. At first, we drove rather quietly both of us engrossed in our own thoughts. Finally, Freddy remarked about the scenic views and the beauty of the area where we were. Then, out of nowhere, "You know there have been some problems with some of the girls over the fact that you come and go as you please."

"Well, I don't think that it's me. I get along pretty well with the girls. I think it's the freedom they want. How did you find out?"

He didn't answer. "Has Codlock had any conversations with you about the new place?" Freddy asked.

"No. He mentioned that he was planning something big and was putting together a team, but we haven't sat down to talk about it yet."

"Yesterday, Codlock, Roy, Dixie, and me got together. Roy and Dixie said that if things didn't improve, they were going to pull their girls out. Either something changes or they're out."

"Well, that fat pig can kiss my ass. No one restricts my freedom, Freddy, no one."

"Listen Sandra, this new place is going to be a big time deal. Codlock has political support for it, which means big volume and bigger money. This kind of shit is not what he needs right now."

I reached into my purse for my flask. "Is this just Norman and Roy? Are any of the other pimps involved?"

"Don't know, but I don't think so. Right now, all I've heard is from those two."

"This is payback for New Year's Eve Freddy; you know that! That pig hates me so much that he would rather get me than get rich. Does that make any sense to you?"

"No, Sandra, but..."

"But, nothing, Freddy. Who's running the show, Codlock or Norman?"

"Down here it works like this. Dixie, Roy, me and the other guys are like independent contractors, not employees, or family, like Chicago. We can pull out whenever we please, but if we stay, we play by Codlock's rules. Right now, he's looking to increase his stable for the new place he's going to open. He doesn't want Roy and Dixie to leave."

"Those girls would be unhappy here or anywhere else. Come on, Freddy, this is just good old boy shit!"

"Sandra, Codlock likes you, you know that. He would never screw you. He wants you as a madam at the new place to teach these young girls to be better, more polished; you know what I mean...more like you."

I saw my opening and I took a chance. "And that's another thing, Freddy. These girls, they're mostly underage. Norman and Roy are recruiting out of state and bringing them across state lines. They are practically slaves, and that's federal shit! You think Codlock has that covered?"

"How old were you when you started?" Freddy asked.

"Twenty-one."

"Slaves, come on," Freddy scoffed. "Look Sandra, down here girls are just different. There's a different kind of relationship between young women and older men, sort of a 'big daddy' thing. If Codlock says he has it covered, he has it covered."

I had my answer. Freddy was no different from the rest of them. "State and local coverage, I'd believe. Anyway, if they're not enslaved, why can't they go out?" I asked.

"Cause they spend money when they go out. Why do you care if you're not transporting them?"

"Don't be stupid, Freddy. I can't teach a girl to be a pro if she's not into it; attitude is everything in this business. You know that. Don't blow off this federal thing, either. If the feds want you, they will get you. If you live in Chicago, you know that, too!"

"Alright, you have some good points; we need a win-win," Freddy mumbled.

"Just drive." I sat in the car as we drove through the mountains. I lit one cigarette after another and stewed. Freddy was quiet. We must have driven for an hour as I went through different scenarios in my mind.

"Pull over here," I asked Freddy as we came to a natural overlook. The sun was out and the air was crisp. The temperature was in the mid-fifties, nice for January. "Hop out." Freddy and I stood overlooking the town of Newport. "I'll give you your win-win."

"What?"

"Codlock's biggest problem isn't me, it's time. As you said, he doesn't need this shit now. I'll give him time, but what we need to do is redefine roles. If Norman and Roy want me out, I'm out. I'll live with you. No more bitching about Sandra. Then we need a meeting where Codlock tells the girls that he's aware of some issues they have and that you, Norman, Roy, and the others have agreed that things will change in the very near future. He can tell them as much or as little as he wants about the new place, dangle the carrot so to speak, but there is to be no more bitching about freedom. He also announces his team and tells them that you and I will be helping in the transition. In the interim, it's business as usual."

Freddy's face lit up. "I like it. Codlock will like it. And, it will make Norman and Roy look bad if they don't go along."

Freddy looked out over the scenery. "We need to have these talks more frequently; you could learn a lot from me, Sandra." He smiled as he wrapped his arm around me and we leaned against the hood of his car, just enjoying the beauty of the valley below and talking details. When we got back to The Court, we met with Codlock and explained the plan.

"So that's the plan. What do you think?" Freddy asked.

114

Codlock smiled, "I like it. It gives me time, but what about you, Sandra, are you okay with this?"

"It's her plan!" Freddy emphasized.

"Is that true?"

"It is if you like it; if you don't, it's all Freddy's," I said as I wrapped my arm around him and smiled.

Codlock gave me that big pumpkin grin of his. "I like it." He held out his arms and walked over to me.

"Before we start hugging and back slapping, shouldn't we find out if Norman and Roy are on board?"

"I'll meet with them tonight," he responded with conviction. "Now, let me lay out this new project we're working on for you."

Codlock went on to explain to me that there was a network of truck stops and houses of prostitution run by a syndicate operating from Florida to Tennessee. The business was primarily prostitution, but they also dealt in drugs and alcohol, illegal guns, and murder for hire. The hierarchy of the organization was similar to The Outfit, but the structure was different. There was no set line of authority. The impression I got was that it was more or less ruled by money, violence, and some good old boys with political juice. My first thoughts were, "I wonder if Marsh knew when he got me involved in all this."

The plan Codlock set out for me was to open a new hotel in Santee, South Carolina. It would be a super truck stop and Motor Inn off I-95 called The Sanctuary Inn. The design was similar to The Court, except this facility would be much larger. While open to the public, the hotel would cater to truckers running on I-95, and become a mid-point for pimps and the trafficking of women up and down the coast. That's where I came in. Codlock thought I could help teach working girls the finer points of our business so that rates and revenue would increase. The plan seemed well thought out, but obviously required political support. I told him I liked the plan. Then, we talked money, lots of money.

The next morning I got up early, showered, dressed, and walked downtown. Since a cold wind was blowing, I wore my new parka. When I got to the store, the smell of fresh brewed coffee filled the air.

"Good morning, Sandra, coffee?"

"Elmer, you silver tongued devil, you talked me right into that." Elmer greeted me with a hug and a kiss; he owned the store. He was in his late fifties, a very nice man with a very nice personality, and one of my regulars at The Court. I walked back to where the coffee sat on a hot plate and poured a cup. Elmer joined me and poured himself a cup. We talked for a while, then he went back behind the counter and I went into the phone booth. I dialed the number and Emma came on the line.

"Hello."

"Hello, Emma. It's Sandra Love, ID 05151940, is Eric there?

"Good morning, Sandra, he's in his room. Wait a minute and I'll get him on the line."

"Hello."

"Eric, it's Sandra."

"What's new, Sandra?"

"Yesterday, the whole thing fell in my lap."

"What do you mean?"

"Codlock and I met; he wants me to coach the new girls, especially the young ones coming in so they'll be more professional and they'll be able to charge more for services rendered. They are planning to open a new facility called The Sanctuary Inn in Santee, South Carolina just off I-95. It will be a mid-point for trafficking up and down the coast. Eric, these guys are organized and have juice. Did you know about this?"

"That's great, Sandra, you've done real well. When are you..."

"You didn't answer my question, Eric," I interrupted him, "Did you know about this?"

"Calm down, Sandra, and I'll tell you. I did not know any of this and I know no one at the agency knew anything about Santee. What we knew was what I told you. We knew there was an organized group of men running under-age girls north across state lines for the purpose of prostitution. We needed more information on the organization; that's where you came in."

"Well, I'm in. I'm in up to my eyeballs now. We need to meet and talk about...HOLY SHIT!"

"What's the matter?"

"Eric, Norman and Roy just walked into the store and they're on their way back here...I got to go!"

"NO! Stay on the line Sandra and calm yourself down. Emma will pick up, she'll be your mother; be cool, I'll be in touch."

I couldn't believe what happened next. Emma picked up the line and started in mid-sentence, "...so we had Tony at the doctor last Wednesday, all his blood work was normal, and he hasn't had a seizure in more than a week."

"What...?"

It was as if I really was talking to my mom! Then Emma asked, "How's the weather down there? Are you getting to wear your new jacket Santa brought you?"

The question was so unexpected, it just stunned the fear right out of me...how did she know?

"I-I-I'm wearing it now...m-mom."

Suddenly, the door of the phone booth opened up. I turned around and there stood Norman with Roy behind him.

"I thought that was you, Sandra. Hey, Roy, it is Sandra!" He yelled without even turning towards Roy.

"Hey, Sandra, what's you up to girl?" Roy asked with a big grin on his face.

"I'm talking to my mother, Roy. Give me a few minutes here and I'll be out." I started to close the booth door, but Norman put his foot in the booth and jammed it open.

"Mind if I say hello to your mom?" Norman asked and stuck out his hand for the phone.

I was fuming; all fear was gone. I got up off the booth seat and stood facing Norman, "Stay cool," I thought. "Hey, mom, a couple of friends just came in and would like to say 'hi'." I handed Norman the phone.

"Sure, honey." I could hear Emma on the other end respond as I handed the phone to Norman.

"Hello, Mrs. Love?"

"Hello, this is Sandra's mother, who am I speaking to?"

"My name is Norman and yours?"

"Well, it's nice to talk to a friend of Sandra's. I'm Helen. I hope you boys are taking real good care of my girl down there?"

"Yes ma'am, we are; we think a whole lot of your Sandra down here." Slowly, that grinning pig lost his smile.

"Well, she's always made friends very easily. Tell me Norman, is she wearing that green Eddie Bauer parka we bought her for Christmas? It's in the teens up here in Chicago; what's the temperature down there in Tennessee?"

"Y-yes ma'am she is...it's not that cold down here. We'll look out for her though." Norman was realizing his mistake. "I got to go so I'm going to put her back on the line. Nice talking to you, ma'am." Norman handed me the phone and I pointed to the door; he closed it. I glared at him through the glass. He looked sheepish.

"Hi, mom, I'm back on now. I have to go, too. Tell dad that I hope we get a chance to talk real soon. Oh, and thanks, you're a great mom!"

Emma responded, "You're a pretty good daughter, too." We hung up.

As I stepped out of the booth, they were retreating towards the front of the store. "Norman!"

They stopped and turned around, "Hey, Sandra, it just pays to be careful in this business."

I knew I had his balls on the block. "I come here to have privacy when I talk to my family; can you understand that?"

"Yea..."

"Don't ever let this happen again understand?"

"Yeah, sorry."

"We have a meeting with Codlock coming up and he's going to make us all rich unless someone screws it up. Then, I think he's going to make someone dead. What do you think, Norman?"

"Yea...you're right." Norman mumbled. He appeared nervous and he started to sweat.

"So you're a team player?"

"Yea..." Norman hung his head, embarrassed.

"Me, too, Sandra," Roy added.

"Good. Now, can you guys give me a lift back to The Court?"

Norman and Roy drove me back to the hotel; there were no further incidents with the pimps.

A few days later Codlock met with the girls and I moved in with Freddy. I'd been to Freddy's home several times. He lived outside Knoxville in a trailer, the biggest singlewide made at the time. The living room, dining room, and kitchen were in the center of the trailer and there were two bedrooms and two full baths. When he bought the trailer, he took out all the furnishings and filled it with solid oak furniture, marble tables, king-size beds, and new plush carpet. He had tastefully arranged his pictures and a crystal chandelier hung over the dining room table. Before I moved in, I made it clear to Freddy that my cat, Jerry Crosby Miller, would come with me. Freddy was okay with that as long as the cat was in my room when we weren't there.

After moving to Freddy's, meeting with Eric Marsh became much easier. He worked out of the FBI's Knoxville Office. I'd have Freddy drive me to a salon in Knoxville and then I'd tell him I'd meet him for lunch or dinner in a few hours. Then, I'd meet with Eric. I briefed Eric on Codlock's plan and he told me that the Santee operation was underway. He felt that if we could get evidence on whoever was behind that operation, we could bust the whole syndicate. We set out a plan that was perfect. Codlock wanted me to meet with each girl and evaluate them, then give both him and their pimp a report. I was to set up a schedule of meetings, times and locations, and the pimps would ensure that their girls got there. All I had to do was give a copy of my schedule to the feds and they saw that the room was bugged. Could it have been any easier?

I spent a few days interviewing the girls. I asked them about their back-stories; where they were from, their age, and how they got into the business. Some of them were pretty seasoned, but most of them were in their teens or early twenties. They had all been told not to enjoy or show any emotion when with a John. Wham, bam, thank you ma'am was the order of the day. I found out later that the pimps felt if the girls showed emotion, they could feel emotion and they did not want anyone falling in love. I reported to Codlock after each interview and the next week there was a meeting with Codlock, the pimps, and me. It was on my schedule...in the ballroom.

We sat at two big round tables, nine at a table. Codlock opened the meeting with a couple of minor items and then he introduced me.

"You all know Sandra. You know her background, and you know what she's done since she came here. In less than a year, our numbers have increased a little over a hundred and twenty percent; that also includes Freddy's business. You are all familiar with our expansion plans; we have an opportunity to do some big business and get rich at the same time...without risk. As you all know, I've asked Sandra to meet with each of your girls and evaluate them. We want to find out how we can improve our product so we can increase our revenue. I want you guys to listen to what she has to say. Sandra."

I stood up and faced the other table. "Thank you, Codlock. I think I've met with each one of you regarding individual girls; you have some real nice and really talented girls working for you. I'm not here to tell you how to run your business. It's your business and you run it as you see fit. What I'm here for is to tell you how I learned my business and why I'm so successful with it. The answer comes down to one word, gentlemen... enthusiasm."

I paused and there was a dead silence in the room. I was comfortable with it and I let it hang out for more than a minute, while I sipped at my coffee, then the whispering started. Finally, Norman could not contain himself any longer.

"Maybe you could tell us what you mean, Sandra."

"I started in the business ten years ago, a hundred dollars a trick. In six months, I was making five hundred a trick. Is that what you want to hear about, Norman?"

"If he doesn't, I do!" shouted one of the other pimps at the other table.

Another one yelled out, "Yeah shut up Dixie or I'll come over there and..."

"Blow me!" Dixie hollered back.

Another pimp shouted, "As soon as Sandra tells us how to get more money, I might just arrange that for ya!"

Everyone in the room laughed, even Norman. When it settled down, I had their attention.

"In my case, the location changed. I went from a hotel in Gary, to the best apartment in Chicago...and the price went up. That's what Codlock is offering you guys; Santee is a step up for all of you."

"Why you, Sandra? How come out of all the girls you got picked?" One of the pimps asked.

"That's an excellent question. The answer is that I had a personal reason that motivated me, a few of your girls have the same reason, but most of the girls have a different reason."

"What's that?" Roy asked.

I picked up my coffee and took another sip. Then, using my mother's pregnant pause, I said, "They love you."

I thought the room was silent before, but this was more like death. Finally, Roy asked, "Are you serious?"

"Of course not, you moron. Who could love anyone as ugly as you guys?"

Everyone in the room busted up, even Codlock. Then they settled down.

"Now, here's the secret, guys," I whispered, "and if you think about it, you'll know I'm right. Go back a minute ago to right after I said, 'They love you.' Remember how you felt, remember the silence in this room? Whether they love you or not does not matter; what matters is the fantasy...the illusion...that's what I sell...and, I am paid very well for making my customers feel like they're loved. Face it guys, if they felt like that all the time, they wouldn't come to see us."

"That's it?" Someone shouted.

"Well, they have to know their way around a man, but that's mechanics. I'm talking about art. Where you guys went wrong is you told them to get rid of the art and focus only on mechanics and if they didn't, you'd beat the crap out of them. Bad form, gentlemen. You have to give them back their enthusiasm."

"She's good, Codlock," One of the pimps at our table said. "Now what?"

"I'm here for you guys, to help this team be the best. If you want me to help you with your girls, see me after the meeting and we'll set something up. Just one thing, guys, I'll see only one girl at a time, at a hundred an hour.

"Yea, but how long does it take?" Norman asked.

"Norman, some will only take an hour, others maybe longer. We will talk after I meet with your girls. Without your help and support, I have no chance. Remember, Norman...team!"

Everyone in the room signed up.

The Outlaw Sandra Love

The Trip to Florida

I had not heard from Robert Allen in almost a month.
Marsh kept reassuring me that he was just taking care
of his family, but I was worried. Codlock arranged for
Freddy and I to go to the Smith Truck Stop outside of
Jacksonville, Florida. This stop was a prepping area
for girls from Georgia, Alabama, and Florida before
they came north. I called Marsh to let him know what
was happening.

Freddy and I packed our bags Sunday night. I took
one evening dress, heels, and some jewelry, and the
rest of my things were casual, sandals, shorts, tops,
and, of course, underwear. We were leaving the next
morning and planned to be away for two weeks.
Freddy had asked one of his girls to come in to take
care of Jerry Crosby Miller. I remember the sun
shining through the window of my room that morning
awakened me. I used to hate that. I dragged myself
out of bed and could smell Freddy's coffee. As I
walked out to the kitchen, Jerry Crosby Miller followed
me; he was now sleeping on my bed at night. I sat
down heavily. Freddy put a mug of coffee and the
sugar bowl in front of me and greeted me with, "Hey!
You look like shit!"

"Go to h... Ah, never mind." I wasn't awake yet.

"Take your time, but I'd like to get on the road by nine,
okay?"

"What time is it?"

"It's a little after eight."

"Give me a half an hour."

"Listen, it's a beautiful morning. I'll cleanup and wait for you outside."

We talked a bit about the trip while I woke up and Freddy cleaned up. Then he left and I showered, brushed my teeth, and did my hair back in a ponytail and stuck it through the back of my Cubs baseball hat. I loved the Cubs' Ernie Banks; 14 times an all star, two MVP's, one Golden Glove, first Chicago player to have his number retired, and this was his last year. As I put on my jeans, I reminisced about games Tony and I had seen. I opened the door of the trailer and there stood Robert Allen leaning up against Freddy's car with a bunch of 'redneck roses' in his hand.

"Hi, Hon."

My damn heart was beating so fast, Robert Allen told me later that the expression on my face was priceless. I composed myself and glared at him. I put my bags down, then I walked over to him, real close, my chest pressed into him just above his belt.

"It's been almost a month and all I get is 'Hi, Hon' and some wildflowers?"

He reached out with those huge arms and enveloped me. He bent over and whispered in my face, "And this." God that man could kiss! He drained every bad thought or feeling out of me in less than a minute.

"You're forgiven," I gasped. To this day, I still don't understand how Robert Allen could get me going so quick, but he sure could. Maybe it was that outdoor smell he had or his huge hands.

"Hello, Sandra."

I turned around and there stood Jerry Crosby Miller, my cat's namesake. Jerry always wore black. He told me that the TV show, "Have Gun-Will Travel" and the gun for hire "Paladin" role Richard Boone played influenced him a lot. He was always nice to me. I think my relationship with Robert Allen influenced Jerry, because when it came to killing people, he had no moral compass at all.

"Hi, Jerry. Did you bring my man over here?"

"Hon, Codlock asked Jerry and me if we'd go with you."

"Hmmm, okay, but you'll have to ride shotgun because Robert Allen and I have dibs on the back seat." I jumped into Robert Allen's arms, and he carried me into the back of the car as Jerry and Freddy put the bags in the trunk. Then, we were off to Florida.

I think I may have told you, I don't talk about my men much, but there is always an exception to every rule, don't you think? I did Robert Allen real good in the back seat of that car and I assure you he returned the favor, twice. Yep! Jerry never said a thing. Freddy turned on the radio, a new group called ZZ Top was playing, and they had real good rhythm. Freddy turned it up louder. It was great music to fuck by.

After awhile, I leaned forward, my cap hanging off the side of my head. "Freddy, what time is it?" I asked.

"Ten minutes to eleven."

"I'm starving, is anyone else hungry? Let's stop and eat, what's the rush?

"Come here!" Robert Allen grabbed me and pulled me back onto the back seat as I screamed and giggled.

"See if you can live on love for a while, Hon. Freddy, if you see a nice place, pull in. Sandra's worked up an appetite."

Robert and I just kissed and snuggled in the back seat. Ten minutes later, we stopped for breakfast.

We arrived at the Smith Truck Stop in Jacksonville around 7pm. It was warm for March. We did not blend. Robert and I wore jeans with light tops, Jerry was in black slacks and a dress shirt, and Freddy wore gray silk slacks and a white shirt with his sleeves rolled. Try to envision the four of us getting out of a white Lincoln Continental at what looked like a bum-fuck Egypt truck stop. I was grateful it was dark.

"You're kidding, right?"

"Shhh, Hon."

"Freddy?"

Freddy was smiling. No wait, sorry, he was snickering.

"Welcome to Florida!" He held both of his arms out in the air and smiled. He started to walk towards the restaurant. He waved his hand for us to follow, "Come on."

Smith Truck Stop had six diesel pumps for trucks alongside the restaurant and six regular gas pumps in front. The building was a one-story hip roof structure made out of wood painted chocolate brown.

Several small windows allowed you to see into the restaurant and there were double glass doors in the middle of the building. We went inside and Freddy turned to the cashier saying, "Table for four."

"Freddy! Freddy LeBlanc!"

"Oh shit! Eileen! How the hell are you?" The cashier, a woman in her mid-forties, got up off her chair, came around the counter, and hugged Freddy like a long lost brother. "What are you doing here?" Freddy asked.

"Well, I sure ain't cashiering, honey." She laughed and turned towards us. "Who are your friends?"

"This is Robert Allen," Freddy started to introduce us.

"Pleased to meet you, Robert Allen, I'm Eileen." She extended her hand and looked him up and down like a cut of meat.

"Eileen," Robert Allen smiled and responded as I envisioned the headline of the local paper tomorrow in my mind, "Local Woman Commits Suicide, Shot in Head Six Times!"

"And this is Sandra Love."

"Oh, honey, we've heard a lot of good things about you. Wish I had met you twenty years ago."

"Thank you, that's very kind of you. It's nice to meet you, Eileen."

"See you're a cubs fan. I grew up in Chicago," she pointed at my hat. "What a shame about Ernie retiring this year."

"Yes, I'll miss him." The local headline in my mind changed suddenly to read, "Local Woman Named Woman of the Year!"

"And this is our friend, Jerry."

Jerry nodded, so did Eileen. Neither spoke.

"Is Harry here?" Freddy asked.

"He's in the office; I'll call him and have him come over. Meanwhile, do you want a table or booth?"

"Table is..." Freddy started to say.

"Booth in the back, thank you, Eileen," Jerry interrupted.

Freddy nodded and Eileen escorted us back to the booth. She took our drink orders and left four menus.

After she left, Robert Allen spoke. "How do you know Eileen, Freddy?"

"She was one of my girls in Leary. She probably works here, too. Why?"

"You two listen up now. We're here because Codlock thinks very highly of the two of you, and he doesn't want to see anything happen to you while you're here, understand?"

"Yes," I said and hugged Robert Allen's arm.

"Absolutely," Freddy followed, "just tell us what you want us to do."

"We don't want to interfere with what you're doing here and we don't want to restrict your movement, but we need to know where you are and where you're going to be. Okay?"

"Sure, you got it." Freddy agreed.

"Sandra?"

"Yes." There was something about Robert Allen that just made me feel protected. With Jerry there, I sort of felt like President Nixon and Jerry was my Secret Service guy.

"Freddy! I haven't seen you since you sold your place in Leary. Jack took a hit on that one, eh. How've you been, you lucky bastard?"

"Hi, Harry. Pull up a chair." Harry Rose was a stout middle-aged man with salt and pepper hair and baggy pants held up by suspenders that crossed his white, short sleeved, rumpled dress shirt.

After Freddy introduced us, Harry asked, "Codlock thinks a great deal of you Sandra. Would you like to see our set up here?"

I got somewhat curious now because I was beginning to think either he had a basement or the girls were working out of the trucks. "That would be nice, Harry, thank you."

"Finish your coffee and I'll change and we'll go over together."

Harry left. Robert Allen turned to Freddy and asked, "Where are we going, Freddy?"

Freddy leaned forward and lowered his voice. "Down here they pay off local cops like we do, but you can't throw it in their face. They want things out of sight. The operation is about a hundred yards down the road behind this building, in the woods. It's an L-shaped motel with eighteen rooms and an office. It's kind of like the Bates Motel in that "Psycho" movie."

"Who will be there?" Robert asked.

"The girls, whoever is taking money, and a bouncer, and maybe a pimp or two, but it's awful early for any of them to be here."

Robert Allen nodded in the direction of the motel and Jerry left.

"Is there a problem?" Freddy asked. He looked worried.

"No, not now," Robert Allen responded quietly. I was beginning to see Robert Allen as he first described himself to me, as a problem solver.

Harry came back and I didn't recognize him at first. In ten minutes, he had shaved and combed his hair, put on a powder blue shirt, kakis pants, and a navy blue blazer. He looked like he was going to a yacht club. He even had on Old Spice.

"Where's Jerry, is he coming?"

"He went on ahead," Robert Allen, answered.

"Oh, that's not good. I have a man up there and he is huge. I can't be responsible for..."

"Don't worry about Jerry, he'll be fine. Ready?"

We got in Freddy's car and drove back to the motel. When we pulled up in front of the office, a huge man was sitting on the step and Jerry was standing behind him. There was another older man standing next to Jerry, talking to him. Jerry was wearing a .357 magnum in a shoulder holster. We got out of the car and Harry asked the big man on the step if he was okay.

"Yeah, but that's a big gun that fella has; I didn't think it was worth arguing with him."

Harry introduced us to Zeke and Guy. When Zeke stood up, I guessed his weight to be around three hundred pounds. Guy was a nice looking older man that worked at the front desk, very personable.

"I got two guest rooms for you all," Harry said. "You can park in front of your room. All of the girls are in and there is a break room behind the office where you can meet with them all together or one at a time. It seats twenty at five tables and standing room. Some of the pimps will be in tonight; all of them will be here tomorrow night at 8pm. Codlock asked me to be there when you meet with the men.

We settled into our rooms and I showered. As I was putting on my panties, Robert said, "Hold on, Hon, I've got a present for you from Eric Marsh." He reached in his bag and pulled out a small recorder with a lead wire and a roll of tape. The recorder was about the size of a watch.

"Robert Allen, when did you see him?"

"Don't get your bustle all rustled, all you need to know is that I saw him and I'm on your side."

I walked over to him and put my arms around his neck. "Where are you going to put that thing?"

"Behave. Put your arms up."

I put my arms up over my head and crossed my wrists like I was tied up. I bowed my head down and stood there in just my panties. "Why do you boys always want to do such nasty old things to me," I cooed.

"Damn, Sandra, knock it off...later."

"Promise?"

"Yes, now what are you wearing?"

I wore an inexpensive knee length dress and a lightweight cardigan sweater. Robert taped it to my ribs on the left side and put the wire in the center of my belly. The tape was good for four hours. We hung out in the break room, and met and talked to a few of the girls. They were all very young, none of them was twenty-one, and most of them were under eighteen. I was surprised at how pretty they were. One of them wanted to know, "Are you the one who worked in Chicago for Al Capone?"

I laughed, "Damn girl," I answered, "I ain't that old!"

Robert Allen laughed.

I met a young girl named Lisa; her story was typical. She had long blonde hair and a nice tan that she told me she got from laying out on towels on the roof of the motel with some of the other girls. She had a voluptuous figure and carried herself well. We sat at one of the tables in the break room and I asked her how she got in the business.

"I met David at a convenience store where I was working as a clerk. He came in every day and was always very polite. One day he asked if I'd like to go to dinner with him and I said yes. I had never dated someone that old before, but I knew he had money from the way he dressed, his jewelry, and the red Corvette he drove.

We went out several times and he took me to nice restaurants and bought me some nice clothes. On our third date, I slept with him. Afterwards, he asked me why I was working at the store. He told me he could get me a job where I could make much more money than I was making at the store. I asked him about the job and he told me flat out it was entertaining men. I'm not the brightest person in the world, but I knew he was talking about prostitution. I asked him how much I could make and he told me twenty-five to thirty thousand dollars a year. I was making a dollar sixty an hour at the store, sixty-four dollars a week, so I brought home a hundred and two dollars every two weeks. David told me I could make that in one night.

"Seems like a lot of money," I commented.

"Listen, Sandra, I was no angel. I took up with boys when I was fourteen. I like sex. David asked me about my background and I told him. He asked me if any of the men I slept with ever paid me? I told him they hadn't."

"Then don't you think it's kind of stupid to be working in that store when there's guys' out there willing to pay big bucks to have sex with you? He asked me. That got me thinking, alright."

"How long before you decided to take him up on it?"

"Well, that was funny; he never mentioned it again. However, a week later, he told me that he was leaving to come to Jacksonville. I asked him if he would take me with him. I was living with my mom and dad, who fight like cats and dogs, and I can tell you that working in the store was not the safest job in the world. I don't understand why people rob convenience stores; they never have very much money."

"So, where are you from?"

"Mobile, Alabama."

"When did you get here?"

"It was just after I turned seventeen, which was last month."

"Are you satisfied with the work?"

"Well, yes and no. I like spending my time off with David because I really love him and I think he loves me too, but I wish he'd tell me how much money we've made. He tells me he's investing the money. He said, "You don't get rich working for money; you get rich when your money works for you." Then he tells me to be patient, saying, "You don't get rich overnight." The other girls tell me that their pimps are doing the same thing, so I guess it's okay. Some of the girls have mean pimps; they get slapped around sometimes...you know what I mean?"

"Yes, I do. Anything else bother you?"

"Well, I don't like having sex with more than one guy a night. Last week I had three in one night and I was really sore. I got my period the next day, so I didn't have to work. When I told David, he responded with, "The more guys, the more money" but he said he didn't want to see me hurt. Sandra, I heard you're going to teach us stuff so we can make more money. Who's your pimp?"

"Well, we're going to try. To answer your question, Lisa...I am my own pimp, but that took a long time."

I talked to two other girls that night, one was eighteen, and the other was nineteen. They worked for other pimps. The one who was eighteen had also come from Alabama when she was underage, but the nineteen-year-old had only been there a couple of weeks and she was from Florida.

Robert Allen and I met with David and another pimp named Nate, the tape was still on. We talked about our visit and the meeting scheduled for the next day. The word was out on our visit. If you wanted to stay at Smith Truck Stop, the meeting was mandatory. We also talked about the organization. I talked about the plans for the future. The pimps talked about their histories, how they got into the business, and how they currently operated. Everything went perfectly. When we got up to leave, I turned around and there was Jerry Crosby Miller sitting in the corner drinking ice water. I remember thinking, "That fits."

"Good night, Jerry." I stopped, bent over, and kissed him on the forehead. "Thank you."

All he said was, "Good night, Sandra."

We got back to the room around 1am. Robert Allen changed the tape and gave it to me. Later in the day, I had Harry set up a rope line in the back of the break room and strung a sheet from it. Eight o'clock rolled around quickly. When Robert Allen, Freddy, and I walked into the break room, Harry and Zeke sat at the first table and Jerry stood behind them. The table had a dozen guns on it.

Robert Allen looked at Jerry and said wryly, "Looks like you're making some new friends down here, partner."

"Precautions." Jerry's face never changed.

I was dressed in the same outfit I wore the night before, but this night Robert Allen wore the wire. I don't think anyone was impressed when we walked in or when Harry introduced me.

I stood up in front of the men, "Thank you, Harry. I've had a chance to talk with some of you regarding our visit. I'm here to talk about the future of this organization and to listen to what you want in the future. If those ends meet, we look forward to you moving on with us, if they don't, you will be free to try to achieve your goals somewhere else. We would like you to stay.

"Sounds good to me, honey, where do I sign up?" One of the pimps shouted out.

"You're already a member; we just want to make sure you stay with us. I'm not here to tell you how to run your business. It's your business and you run it as you see fit. What I'm here to tell you is the direction our organization is taking and to make sure you understand how to board the train when we leave."

"We're all going north, is that it?" One of them asked.

"No, we're all getting rich, that's it." I responded.

"I'd like to see that, honey?"

"You would? Well, how about the rest of you? Would you like to see that tonight?"

The men started shouting and whistling and after a minute, they settled down. I held two fingers up in the air. "If you gentlemen will give little old me just two minutes, I'll show you what that looks like. Can someone time me?"

"I will!" Harry called out.

I walked over to the sheet that Harry had hung in the back of the room and turned. I put my two fingers up in the air and blew the men a kiss, then stepped behind the curtain. The talking started immediately. I stripped off the sweater, dress, and sandals.

Harry called out, "thirty seconds!"

I put on a black push up bra that matched my panties, a black garter belt, and coffee-colored nylons.

"One minute!"

I slipped my little black dress over my head and zipped up the side, adjusted my breasts, and stepped into my heels as I let my hair down and brushed it out.

"Ninety seconds!" The shouting grew louder.

I powdered my face and put on some lipstick.

"Ten, nine, eight, seven," Everyone in the room was counting.

I turned towards the curtain, took a deep breath, and grabbed the right edge of the curtain with my left hand. My last thought was, "At least you learned something at The Coral Club. Now smile!"

I tore the sheet back and struck a pose. There was a few seconds of silence and then applause. When Ernie Banks retired later that year, he received a standing ovation from the crowd at Wrigley Field...this was mine. I walked around the room stopping in front of each man and bending over so he could see my cleavage while I lifted my skirt up to the top of my nylons.

Guess they liked what they saw; everyone wanted to get rich.

Sudden Death

In the next ten days, we met with the pimps and the rest of the girls. Some of the pimps told us that they were also involved in running guns or selling drugs as well as trafficking women. Robert Allen bought a M1911 colt .45 with two full clips and a dime bag of weed. He said he bought it just to get it on the record, but he smoked some of the weed on our way home and kept telling me how "cherry" the gun was.

During the meetings, I'd get the ages of the girls and who and when they were brought to Jacksonville. After that, I would stress to them the importance of creating a fantasy for each customer along with the mechanics of the sex. With the pimps, I would get them to confirm what the girls had told me and then emphasized the importance of their role in making each of their girls the best they could be so that they could increase their price. It worked like a charm. We left Jacksonville and got back to Newport on Friday March 5th. I told Freddy that I was going to spend the weekend at Robert Allen's, but Saturday afternoon we met with Eric Marsh and gave him the tapes. We told him what was on the tapes.

He thought about it for a moment and then responded, "If these tapes have what you say they have on them, we can bust these guys any time we want."

"Speaking of time, I've done this for almost a year. You seemed happy with the Newport meeting tapes, so if you have those up here and these tapes from down there, what more do you need? When do I get out?"

"You've done well, Sandra. From what we've learned, we know that the moneymen will be at the opening of the Sanctuary that's scheduled to open next year. I won't hold you beyond that."

"Okay, two years with the feds will look good on my resume," I told him. "There's a light at the end of the tunnel," I thought. "I can do twelve months standing on my head." Little did I know that the next year would begin my trip into hell!

When we got back to Robert Allen's, there was a 1966 Super Sport Chevelle Malibu Convertible in front of his trailer. It was light blue with a black top and had magnesium wheels. That Chevelle was polished to a tee.

"Robert Allen, looks like you got company," I said as I got out of his truck.

He reached in his shirt pocket and pulled out a set of keys, "I hope so, Hon, for a long time." He smiled.

"No, you didn't!" I ran over to the car, then I ran back to Robert Allen and he picked me up and spun me around as I screamed and then planted a lip lock on him he soon would not forget.

"Can we drive it?"

"Well, I hope so; I worked hard enough on it."

I held out my hand, "Keys please."

It had a big 396cc engine in it and an automatic transmission. As I drove it out on the road, Robert Allen explained how he had adjusted the suspension of the car similarly to the suspensions in the cars he had fixed for moonshiners. He told me no one could ever catch me if I learned how to drive it properly. I didn't understand all the other changes he made to the engine and the carburetor, but I nodded as if I did and told him I thought it was "cherry." He laughed. It was a great weekend.

The following week I moved in with Robert Allen who had spent the better part of the week building a house for Jerry Crosby Miller, the cat. It was three stories tall with cedar shingles on the roof. It had a scratch post outside, a litter box on the first floor, food, and water on the second floor and a bed on the third floor. There were steps in between each floor. It was mounted on plywood. I know it weighed close to twenty pounds.

Robert Allen wanted me to meet his parents who lived in Jones Cove about fifteen miles south of Newport. We visited his parents and I was well-received even though they knew how I earned my living. The more time I spent with Robert Allen the more I fell in love with him, but he had a dark side, too. One night he took a picture off the wall of the trailer, behind it he opened a hidden panel. Inside, it was full of guns, rifles, knives, and ammunition. He wanted me to know this was here just in case I ever needed it. It was very clear that violence was part of his business and he made no qualms about it.

When Freddy and I met with Codlock that week, I told him that I had moved in with Robert Allen. He was fine with that. Codlock told us that Harry had called and that the pimps in Jacksonville wanted to know how many girls they could place in this new facility when it opens up. He seemed very happy. Then he asked Freddy and me if we would make a presentation at the last facility in the organization, a truck stop on I-40 near the North Carolina border.

I took the L sisters, Linda, Lola, and Lilly for a ride in my new car. Over lunch, they filled me in on what was going on at The Court. They told me that there had been trouble with a couple of my regulars; my Jake and Charlie Mueller had gotten physical with Norman and Roy accusing them of beating me. Jake was upset; he hadn't seen me in weeks. Codlock had to intervene on Norman's behalf assuring Jake that everything was okay. We had a ball. On the way back, I pulled up next to Charlie Mueller while he was at a traffic light; his cab was empty.

"Hey, Charlie!" We all yelled and acted like schoolgirls.

"Sandra! You're back! Nice car, is it yours?"

"No!" Linda shouted, "We stole it and now we're going to rob the bank and go to Mexico."

"Yeah, to Mexico! Viva Mexico!" Lola and Lilly were in rare form shouting and hollering with the top down.

"Charlie, can you call Jake and tell him I'll see him this afternoon at The Court at 4pm."

"Sure Sandra." Charlie gave me a thumbs up and I hit the gas as the light turned green. We drove around and stopped at a couple of stores to shop. Then we went back to The Court. I got my room key, and went into The Coffee Shoppe. Codlock was sitting at the counter, next to my Jake.

"Hey, you!" I cried.

Jake shook Codlock's hand, "Thanks, sorry about the trouble."

I snuggled up to him and asked, "Should I be calling you Sugar Ray Jake?"

"Let's go." Jake was always short on words and long on action.

We went up to my room. Jake followed me in and locked the door. He turned around, and in one continuous motion pulled his jean jacket and white T-shirt up over his head and threw them on the chair beside the table. Damn! That boy had the nicest body and his thick dark hair, chiseled jaw, and tan skin were the gravy on the potatoes. My Jake had the complete package and he was getting ready to show it to me as he began to unbuckle his belt.

"Wait a minute!" Jake looked up, "Hi?"

"Oh, I'm sorry, Sandra." Jake walked over and put his arms around me, "I missed you."

"Yeah, I can tell," I whispered, as his erect penis strained against his jeans and me. I reached down and unbuckled his belt and jeans and then I pulled. His jeans dropped to the floor over his tiny bubble butt and he stood there in all his glory. My Jake was not wearing underpants.

He picked me up and lay me on the bed. He kicked off his shoes, stepped out of his jeans, and lay down beside me. Gently, I arched my back and my neck, closed my eyes, and parted my lips slightly. I called the position 'The Invitation'. It was part of the fantasy I created for my clients. Jake, like so many men, loved to undress me. The secret is for you to get excited as he does it. No moaning like a porn movie, that's crap. The key is to be subtle, never rush. We made it twice and then Jake just wanted to talk.

"I know you could never have feelings for me, Sandra, but I like you very much. If the new job you have is going to take you away, will you tell me before you go? That's all I'd ask."

"Yes, I promise, but I'm back now and should be here until next year, okay?" I kissed Jake on the mouth, something I rarely did with a client.

I picked up a pizza and popcorn on the way to Robert Allen's place. We had dinner and a movie at home. I fell asleep in his arms. The next few weeks had me settling back in at The Court. My time was spent between my customers and helping pimps at The Court. The whole atmosphere had changed; even Norman and Roy took their girls out once or twice a week. Everyone was talking about the new place that was going to open next year. I also fielded calls from The Smith Truck Stop pimps, so many that Eric Marsh had the lines tapped. The money I was paid allowed me to cut back on the number of clients I saw, just regulars now. That made both the girls at The Court and Robert Allen happy campers...me too.

******

Mike McLeod was the front boss for the I-40 Truck Stop. Though small in stature, Mike was very muscular. His disposition was short-tempered and mean. He was in his early forties. The real boss was his uncle Codlock, a silent partner so to speak, and whoever the money boys were behind him. Codlock's older brother John, Mike's father, had been killed in an automobile accident while the two of them were running moonshine many years before; Codlock had been driving. After that, he had sworn to take care of his nephew and had set him up at the I-40.

The I-40 Truck Stop had pumps outside for cars and trucks, a clean modern bar, and restaurant and six trailers set up out back each with three bedrooms where the working girls lived and entertained customers. Freddy and I went over to Mike's place in April. At first, he was rather accepting of us being

148

there, but as we spent more time at the I-40 Truck Stop, we found out that the girls were afraid to talk to us. When we met with the pimps, we met individually with them; there was no general meeting of the group. I didn't tape a thing. We were out in two days. On the way home, Freddy and I talked.

"What was your take on that?" I asked him.

"In a word, hostile. For some reason the pimps weren't buying what we were selling."

"I noticed one thing that was different."

"Which was...?"

"Mike. Not negative, but certainly not positive or supportive."

"Yea," Freddy said, "What do you make of that? The train left Mike at the station?"

"No, Mike's on a different train."

"Do we tell Codlock?"

"It's not do we tell Codlock, it's how we tell Codlock. It's his kin."

I remembered something that Jackie Kramer, the attorney in Chicago told me about testifying, "If you want to appear neutral, describe the behavior, and don't characterize it." I shared this with Freddy before we met with Codlock; we went in very low key.

"Hey, you two, come on in. You're back early." Codlock pushed his chair back from his desk and came around it, and greeted me with his normal bear hug and air kiss. "Close the door, Freddy. What are you drinking, Sandra, vodka and tonic... hold the tonic, right?"

"I'll take just a small one, Codlock." I sat down in one of the two leather chairs in front of Codlock's desk and lit a cigarette. I put the match in the floor ashtray that stood between the two chairs.

"Freddy?"

"I'll take Crown and seven, light on the seven, thanks."

As Codlock was fixing the drinks, he asked, "So, how did it go?"

"It was fine," Freddy said as he smoked and looked at me.

"Fine, eh?" Codlock brought Freddy's drink around and handed it to him. Then he brought mine over to me. "Sandra?"

"Thank you." I took mine, straight vodka on the rocks in a tumbler glass, and drank it. I leaned forward and put the empty glass on Codlock's desk as he sat down in his chair. He looked at the empty glass and then he looked at me; I smiled at him. He smiled back, with a look of awareness you rarely see in a man's eyes.

"Fine?" He asked as he stared at me.

"It was fine, but it wasn't exactly the same as here or Jacksonville."

"Fine, eh. Hmmm..." He paused, "Sandra, I'm not very good at guessing games. When it comes to my business, I don't like to beat around the bush. So would you just tell me what the hell happened?"

"Well, I'd say the interviews with the girls were shorter. Would you agree with that, Freddy?"

"Yes, I would. I think that there was a couple that didn't last fifteen minutes."

"And the meeting with the men?" Codlock asked.

"There wasn't any meeting with the men." "Mike wanted us to talk to them one on one."

"That little bastard, I specifically told him a group meeting with everyone there."

The room was silent for a while. Finally, I asked, "Have you talked to Mike today, any feedback?"

"No. I'll give him some time to call; time may be a good thing here." Codlock was pissed and it showed. The room was quiet for a while and then he said, "You guys have done a good job so far. This will all work out. I have a couple of phone calls to make. Take some time off; let's talk again Monday at lunch, noon okay?"

"Sounds good," I said. I knew when I was being dismissed. Freddy and I left. In the parking lot, I told him, "I think it's a good idea to steer clear of Codlock until Monday."

"Yeah, let him chew on it awhile. Enjoy your weekend."

When I got back to Robert Allen's, I called home to touch base with Tony. Mrs. Lewis was having a couple of boys in for a sleepover. Tony caught me up on school events and asked how I was doing. I told him about my new car and when I told him that I thought this job would end next year and I would be home to start our new life together, he was thrilled. We made plans to get together for summer vacation.

******

The next day was Saturday and Robert Allen took me out for dinner. Later we went to a bar out in the country a few miles from Newport. It was a rather notorious bar where there seemed to be at least one shooting every week. It was called The Smokey Mountain Club and was owned by a guy named Joel Cole. Robert Allen introduced me.

"It's nice to meet you, Sandra, I've heard a lot about you."

"All good, I hope."

"Yes, ma'am." His grin was more like a leer.

It was around 9pm and the place was full. Customers stood around laughing, talking, drinking beer, and playing pool at the two tables. I know what you're thinking; you thought the county was dry. It was, so if someone with enough clout came into the bar, folks would just say they brought their own liquor, but no one had to worry about that because it never happened. Joel Cole was not a trusting man. He covered his ass twice. He listed his establishment as a social club with a one dollar membership fee, which made it exempt from the dry law.

Along the walls men sat in booths talking and celebrating the weekend. There was a jukebox to the right when you came in. At the far end of the bar, there was a TV in the corner over the bar. Some of the men were watching a ball game, but I had no interest in it.

Sudden Death

There were no vacant seats so Robert Allen and I saddled up to the bar. He asked if I wanted a beer. I was used to drinking the hard stuff, but told him to order me one.

As I surveyed the scene, I realized I was one of three women in the entire bar; the other two were waitresses. That was just as well. Sometimes a woman, regardless of her looks, can get men riled up especially after they have downed a few beers. I wasn't worried though, because Robert Allen had a reputation of being deadly when crossed and most men in the bar knew him.

I was curious as to why Robert Allen had wanted to come to this particular bar, or any bar for that matter, because he really didn't care much for drinking.

"Why did you want to come here? I asked.

"I have my reasons," he said.

That bothered me. I wondered if there was going to be trouble. I knew he had a gun, but so did most of the other men in the bar. That's when I realized I could wind up in the middle of a shoot-out.

After another round of beer, Robert Allen worked his way around the bar, talking to first one man and then another. He decided to play a game of pool in the poolroom so I went with him to watch. One of the men in the room offered me his stool and I sat down. Around ten that night, a man walked up to Robert Allen and whispered something in his ear. He handed his cue to another man, walked over to me, and said, "Come on, let's go." He offered me his left hand and we started to walk out of the bar hand in hand.

As we passed the man on the last bar stool, Robert Allen let go of my hand and turned towards the bar.

He pulled the Buck knife I gave him for Christmas out of his belt, reached over and grabbed the man around his face, pulled his head back and slit his throat from ear to ear. Maybe two other men saw what happened; it happened that fast. As the man dropped to the floor, Robert Allen turned around saying, "Come on, Hon."

He pushed me towards the door and never looked behind him; the knife was still in his hand. On the way to the truck, he took out a red handkerchief he carried in his pocket and wiped it off. Then we got in the truck and drove away.

I did not say a thing. I was too stunned to speak and my heart was racing. I lit a cigarette and then turned to Robert Allen, "Do you want to tell me about that? Why did you kill that guy? The place was full of witnesses. Who was he?"

"That little bastard was Adam Jones. He was the biggest thief in the county, but he only stole from old people. A few weeks ago, one of my parents' neighbors was robbed and the husband, who was in his seventies, was beaten. We all knew who did it. I had a little talk with Adam about his line of work and he retaliated by spreading some nasty rumors about me that could get me killed. He told some moonshine boys I was working undercover for the feds. He told the wrong guys; they told me! If I had not taken care of him, some folks just might think he was telling the truth. Now, would anyone working for the feds kill somebody in cold blood with all those witnesses?"

"What about the law? Won't they come after you?"

"No, no one would dare finger me. It's just how it is here, Sandra; you don't rat. Don't worry, he won't be missed."

"What will they do with the body, turn it over to his family?"

"I don't know. Joel will take care of it. Maybe they'll take it to that drop off in the mountains I showed you. There's been many a man killed in a bar that ended up at the bottom of that ravine."

I reached down on the floor of the truck and picked up my flask. I took a long drink of vodka; I wanted the nightmare in my head to go away.

The Ambush

April 17th, 1971, was a Saturday and I was off; I had my period. Robert Allen was visiting his parents. It was my first day and I don't have to explain to anyone that has been on the pill what 'heavy flow' means...it means bitchy! It was early evening and I was watching TV, lounging in panties and a T-shirt when the phone rang. I let it ring six times before I answered it.

"Sandra, this is Freddy. I'm in trouble. Can you meet me at my trailer; I can be there in about an hour."

"Oh my Lord, what's wrong?"

"I'll tell you when I see you. Can you come now, please?"

"I'll meet you there at 9pm."

I pulled on a pair of jeans, my leather jacket, and sneakers. I picked up my car keys, threw my flask in my purse, and headed for the door. Then I thought I'd better take my pistol. I opened the bottom bureau drawer and pulled the gun out from beneath my underwear. I was shaking as I loaded it. I stuffed it in my purse, took a long swig from the flask, and ran down the steps to the car.

I tried not to speed as I drove the twenty miles to Freddy's place. On the way, I took a couple of sips of vodka to steady my nerves. I kept thinking about Freddy. Had someone put a hit out on him?

I cut the lights as I turned onto Freddy's road. I parked about fifty yards from his trailer and turned off the engine. It was a bit before 9pm, but it was not totally, dark. A full moon was out and cast an eerie light through the clear starlit sky on the woods. I took the pistol out of my purse and released the safety. I got out of the car and walked as quietly as I could about half way between the car and Freddy's. I could see the trailer, no lights were on and Freddy's Lincoln was not there.

I waited impatiently for Freddy. When ten or fifteen minutes passed and he still hadn't shown I thought, "Where the hell is he?" I was getting pretty cold as the temperature was in the 50's.

When another fifteen minutes passed and Freddy still wasn't there, I decided to head for the trailer. Slowly and quietly, I walked through the woods until I got to his lot. When I stepped out of the woods and into the cleared lot, the moon made everything brighter. I hunched over and crept around to the back door. Freddy kept a key under a flowerpot. I got the key, unlocked the back door, and went into the trailer. It was warm inside; I listened a few seconds, and then tiptoed toward the living room. With the moonlight filtering through the thin curtains and knowing the trailer layout, I made my way past the dining room table and through the living room toward the front door so I could turn on the lights. Just as I reached the front door, I heard a "creaking" noise.

I turned to my left and saw the bathroom door open up, then, I saw a long-barreled pistol come out from behind the door. Scared shitless, I wheeled and raced into the other bedroom where I had stayed when I lived with Freddy.

The Ambush

I heard the bathroom door close behind me and I knew that it closed before I was clear of the hall. "Shit...shit...shit and shit!" I thought. "I'm dead!"

My mind raced; I was so scared that I didn't even close the door behind me. What could I do; I was trapped.

I was on the verge of tears when I realized I had my gun in my hand; this is what Robert Allen had trained me to do! I looked at the bed and then to my right, at the closet. I crept over and opened it. I thought about crawling inside and closing the door thinking maybe all of this horror would go away, but then, I would be trapped inside. I stepped back; there was about two feet between the bed and the outside wall. I left the closet door open, got down on the floor between the bed and the wall, and pointed my gun at the door.

I waited and waited. Nothing. I did not hear a thing. Then slowly and silently, like a black ghost a figure moved into the room. He never made a sound. I could hear Robert Allen's voice in my mind, "Never point a gun at someone, and not shoot it. The first shot is the most important thing about firing a gun to kill."

The figure turned that big gun in front of him right past me; he couldn't see me in the dark corner! He moved toward the closet door. I could feel a bead of sweat run down my forehead as he came closer. I took a breath and raised my gun as if he were a target on a tree. He must have seen the movement because he spun around towards me and then, I fired.

I saw the flames come out of the end of his gun in the dark, but I just kept on pulling the trigger. As my gun fired, I could see the flashes in the dark and the figure fell back against the closet door, pitched to his right and then dropped to the floor as I pulled the trigger over and over again; my gun was already empty.

I could make out his figure on the floor in front of me, I kept my gun trained on him and pulled the trigger a couple of more times before I realized it was empty. He hadn't moved and he was only a few feet from my feet. After a few moments I thought, "Did I get him? I got him!" I went to get up...

"AIEEEEEEEEEEEE..." I screamed in agony, tears came to my eyes.

The pain in my left shoulder was excruciating! "I've been shot." I thought. I laid the pistol on the floor and very gently touched my left shoulder with my right hand; blood covered my hand. "You bastard! Rot in hell you fucking bastard!" I yelled and then I started to cry. "I'm shot...what if I bleed to death? I have to get out of here."

My left arm was useless. I turned to my right and pushed myself up with my right hand onto my knees. One at a time, I pulled my legs underneath me, and stood up wobbling and dizzy. My body quivered for a few seconds and then I pitched forward onto the bed, out cold.

For the next few minutes, I drifted in and out of consciousness. I heard a siren. When I came to, the lights were on and medics surrounded me. One was cutting my shirt off. I turned my head and saw a man propped up in the corner with blood trickling out of his mouth. His left eye was gone and there were other bullet holes in his chest. The medics were working on him, but soon gave up. He was dead. My bullets had found their mark.

The Ambush

I had a huge gauze pad taped on my shoulder and an IV in my arm. I don't remember them doing either. I was lifted onto a stretcher, strapped down, and carried out to an ambulance. On the way out, I saw four or five police officers inside and outside the trailer. After I was inside the ambulance, I realized they were going to put the dead man in the ambulance with me.

"That son-of-a-bitch is not riding with me," I said.

"He has to be taken to the hospital so he can be pronounced dead by a doctor," said one of the medics.

"That son-of-a-bitch shot me. He's dead. Just leave him here and send another ambulance after him."

The medics continued to put the stretcher with the body bag on it into the ambulance. I was determined the dead man was not going to ride with me and began struggling against the straps.

"Damn it! Let me up from here," I shouted. "I'm not riding with that bastard." I started crying.

"Okay, okay just settle down," one of them said. "Take him off Lonnie."

The medics gave up and took the dead man in the body bag out of the ambulance.

At one point during the ride, I said to the medic sitting next to me, "Please, if I'm going to die I want to give you some phone numbers and names."

"You're going to be alright honey. Just tell me what type of blood you have. Do you know?"

"B negative."

"Okay," he said. "I'm going to have to radio ahead and see if the hospital has enough on hand."

At St. Mary's Catholic Hospital in Knoxville, we rushed into the emergency room where the doctors and nurses started working on me. They hooked me up to a monitor, suctioned blood and mucous from my throat and examined the bullet's entrance and exit wounds. I got a shot of morphine and the pain dissipated. They put an oxygen mask over my face and gave me a transfusion; I think they also washed out the wound. One of the doctors said, "There's nothing else we can do until they get here."

They wheeled me into a dark room and I laid there for a while. I didn't know if it was five minutes or five hours, I was so groggy, but even as screwed up as I was I still was worried and I began to get angry. Finally, I got up off the bed and walked out into the hall with my IV tube in tow. One of the nurses came running as soon as she saw me.

"No, honey, you shouldn't be out here, let me help you."

"Look," I said. "If I'm going to die, you should send for a preacher or somebody for me to talk to. I have a son and I want to t-talk to him..." I started crying again as I thought about my Tony. One of the male aides caught up with us and they helped me back into the room. "Could you send a nurse to hold my hand and could I have some water? Could I have a tissue, too, please?" I may have been a bit out of it.

The nurse said, "We have your condition stabilized. You're not going to die. We put you in there because we're waiting for an orthopedic surgeon to come and examine you and we wanted you to get some rest.

Things are pretty quiet now; I'll get you a tissue and a water swab."

They took me back to bed and the nurse looked at the bed. The sheets were covered in blood. She looked at my shoulder and back at the bed. "Honey, are you menstruating?"

I looked at the bed, "I'm sorry," I said. They sat me in a chair and the aide went out and came back with new bedding and a feminine pad. The nurse cleaned me up and got me back in bed. She sat and held my hand.

I drifted off into a fitful sleep. Suddenly bright lights were shining in my face and two nice-looking men in white coats were standing over me. I was lying on my right side. "Who are you?" I asked groggily.

"We're orthopedic surgeons and we'll be examining you," said one of the doctors. "I'm Dr. Lansky and this is Dr. Barnes. We're going to raise the bed up; can you turn and lie flat on your back for us?"

I thought to myself, "Put the money on the nightstand and I'm all yours doc." Instead, I said, "Yes, I think so."

Dr. Lansky removed the dressing from my wound.

"The entry wound is above the collarbone just to the right of the left arm socket," he said to Dr. Barnes.

"Where were you when you were shot and what happened immediately afterward?" asked Dr. Barnes.

"I was backed into a corner in the front bedroom of my friend's trailer and some bastard shot me with a long-barreled pistol. He was standing up and I was sitting on the floor, hiding behind the bed."

"That explains the angle of the wound. I understand you managed to get off a few shots yourself that killed your assailant."

"Yes, I did. It was self-defense."

"That's a police matter," Dr. Barnes said. "We're just concerned with your recovery. Can you raise your left arm?"

I tried, but I couldn't do it. I could not even move it from side to side.

"It appears the bullet damaged your brachial plexus, "Dr. Lansky said. " We are going to take you into surgery this evening and get you sewn up. You'll be admitted."

"I-I don't have any insurance."

"Well, that's why we have something called The Hill-Burton Act. We do not want you worried about money; you just concentrate on getting well. How's that sound?"

"Okay...thank you."

"Someone will come for you in a little while and we'll see you in the OR."

I smiled. I really don't remember much more. After the surgery, they put me in the orthopedic ward, in a semi-private room. I was on pain medication and physical therapy. After I got to feeling better, I'd visit the other patients and sometimes they would ask me to read to them. Some were in really bad shape, mostly from automobile accidents or accidents at work. They had a lot of broken bones; some were in traction and couldn't get up at all.

The Ambush

During my two-week stay, I had a couple of visits from the local law enforcement. I told them what I remembered and they didn't file any charges against me. By the middle of the first week, I started getting visitors. The first one was Codlock.

"Hi, Sandra, how are you feeling?"

I looked up and there was that big bearded face smiling down at me as he held a dozen red roses in a vase. "Well, look who's come a courting." I said.

Codlock bent over and gave me a hug, then, he gave me a Get Well card signed by just about everyone I had ever met in Tennessee, pimps, girls, staff, and clients. It was nice. Then he started talking, make that whispering, as he pulled one of the chairs alongside of my bed.

"Robert Allen, Freddy, and me had a talk Sunday night. Seems Freddy's old partner Jack got out of jail and ran into Harry. Harry mentioned he'd seen Freddy and Jack asked about him. A couple of days later word was out that Jack had put a hit out on Freddy for five thousand. Harry called Freddy last Saturday; the hit man had already left Florida to come here."

"Oh, Freddy must feel really bad."

"He did after Robert Allen was through with him."

"Oh, God, is Freddy alright?" I whispered.

"He's not quite as pretty as he used to be, but he'll be alright. When you get out of here, you are going to live with Freddy for a while. Freddy is going to take real good care of you, believe me. I have never seen a man as angry as Robert Allen was Sunday night."

"I don't want to live with Freddy; I want to live with Robert Allen."

"Honey, it's already done. You're moved, cat and all."

"No, Codlock, what if Jack sends another hit man up here. I don't want to be at Freddy's."

"Shhh..." Codlock put his finger up to his mouth. "Robert Allen sent Jerry Crosby Miller to Florida on Monday. He called last night. You won't be seeing Jack around any more."

I knew exactly what that meant.

"You take some time off; now, you are Freddy's responsibility. If anything else happens to you, it's Freddy's ass, understand?"

"Yes."

"Now Sandra, this is very important. Is there anyone in Chicago that I need to talk to? We don't want any trouble from this."

"I'll take care of it today," I bluffed.

"Thank you. If there's anything you need, anything, you call me, understand?"

"Yes, daddy," I cooed.

Codlock looked down at me. "Yep! You're going to be alright."

******

Agents Marsh and Holt both came to visit me. They came after hours, around 9:30pm. When I told them what Codlock had told me, they seemed surprised.

They thought Mike McLeod had hired the hit man. That surprised me. I asked them why they thought that and they told me there was some bad blood between Mike and Codlock over the death of Mike's father. I hadn't asked Codlock about how things were between him and Mike. A few days later, the agents confirmed the hit man was from Florida.

The following Saturday night around 8pm, I was getting ready to watch Humphrey Bogart in Casablanca on TV when I smelled popcorn. I looked up and there was Robert Allen with a big brown bag of popcorn and two bottles of soda.

I turned my head away and started to cry. He walked over and said, "Please, Hon, don't cry, my popcorn ain't that bad is it?"

I smiled and sniveled, then, he bent over and kissed me. I hugged him with my one good arm and cried for a minute or two. Those big paws held me so I knew nothing could ever hurt me. Then he said, "You did good Sandra, you did real good, Hon."

He filled me in on the move to Freddy's. Freddy's payback for calling me was he now had to take care of me, do things, and be there in a way that Robert Allen couldn't be. I understood. Robert Allen lay down on the bed with me and held the popcorn while we watched the movie and talked during commercials. He came to see me every night after that. The last night he came in, he said something really eerie, "I need you to be strong Sandra; can you be strong?"

"My mother's words again." I thought. "Yes, now go," I told him.

The day I was discharged, I was watching TV when I heard a voice say, "Hi Sandra, I've come to get you. I bought you a new little dress for you to wear home." I turned my head and there stood Freddy LeBlanc.

"Oh Freddy, did Robert Allen do that?"

Freddy had the remnants of a black eye; you know that purple and yellow color around his left eye.

"Yea, guess I took one for the team."

We left the hospital and went to his place. That evening I asked him if he had known the man I killed.

"No, I have no idea who he was."

"Well, tell me what happened that night? Why didn't you show up?"

"I did, but it was too late. I heard the shots just as I parked beside your car. I was the one that called the police and the ambulance. I'm so sorry you got hurt, Sugar, but I'll make it up to you."

Freddy had erased every trace of the shooting in the trailer. Someone had replaced the rug in the bedroom, and scrubbed and painted the walls. It didn't bother me that I was living in the place where I'd been shot and killed a man. Freddy waited on me day and night. I tried to be as appreciative of the care as possible, but I was still taking pain medicine so I could be more aggressive with my physical therapy and it doped me up a lot.

 The one good thing that came out of all this was that I did stop drinking. I guess I didn't need it.

Billy Arrowood

The first few weeks Freddy would wake me up every morning at 7am and make me get up. Then, he would help me shower and dress and he even bought me several outfits to wear when I went to my PT. At first, all I had to do was hold a broom in both hands, raise both my arms up and over my head and then side to side for a few sets. This was to improve my range of motion. After a few weeks, they gave me big bands of elastic that I had to wedge in a doorjamb then use my arms to stretch out the bands.

Freddy bought me a membership at a gym in Knoxville and as soon as I was able to drive, I started working out. I liked weight training and forced myself to lift weights to strengthen my chest, shoulders, and arms. For my legs, I ran on a treadmill. By June, I was really feeling good and I started to resume some normal activity. I would stop by The Court a couple of times a week. Codlock really seemed to like the Latex gym outfits I wore. I met with him and he insisted that I take the summer off to concentrate on rehabbing. He was very generous about it, saying he owed me one from New Years Eve, or maybe it was the gym outfits. I never really knew.

I met my best friend for the first time following one of my gym visits. Billy Arrowood was a well-built, hard-cut man. He reminded me of the actor Charles Bronson. He had long dark hair, light brown skin, dark eyes, and an inner peace that few of us ever achieve. I remember Grayson telling me about his martial arts instructors when I worked at the hotel in Gary. He called them *sensei,* Japanese for teacher. He said that they always seemed to have an inner peace about them, a balance they had achieved in their lives. Billy was not Japanese, he was Cherokee, but he had found that balance.

Billy was in his late thirties and he neither smoked nor drank, but he did walk. He frequently hiked alone in the Smokey Mountains. He went there for solace and had been hiking there for many years. He didn't belong to the gym, but I saw him a few times walking the road to the gym. One day I was coming back from the gym and Billy was walking along the side of the road in the middle of a severe thunderstorm. It was a warm summer day, but the rain was coming sideways. I stopped, leaned across the front seat, and rolled down my passenger side window.

"Can I give you a lift?"

"Sure, thank you," he said as he opened the door and got in. He was drenched to the bone, but he didn't seem to realize he was wet. He didn't even wipe his face off as the water ran down it in little rivulets.

"Would you mind rolling that window back up?" I asked.

"Oh...yes, I can." Billy rolled up the window. He had the softest voice I ever heard on a man, soft, and deep, not feminine.

"Where are you going?" I asked him.

"Wherever you take me, now," He replied. He never looked over at me; he just stared out through the windshield.

That was Billy.

I took him to lunch. We spent the afternoon talking. I told him about what I did for a living and about being shot. He told me that everyone in the area knew the story about the prostitute who killed the assassin. He said he was pleased to meet me. He was one of the few men I was close to that never asked me to go to bed with him. That gave me balance.

Billy made a living doing odd jobs. In the south there is a saying, "A good man can make a decent living in any town if he's willing to work and has a pickup truck." Billy had a pickup that he kept at his home when he wasn't working. He lived in a cabin in the woods that his parents had lived in. A drunk driver killed them in an automobile accident when he was a teen; he had no other family that I knew of. He was a very spiritual man and he often talked about the afterlife.

Billy loved hiking. He began to take me on his mountain hikes. It got so I would spend a day or two a week exploring the mountains with him. Most of the time, we hiked past Del Rio to Round Mountain in Great Smoky Mountain National Park. There was an old bootlegger trail, and a dirt road, that wound round and round the mountain and ran between Hot Springs, North Carolina and Newport, Tennessee.

We took very little with us. Billy would bring his shotgun or his .30-30 rifle or his forty-pound re-curve bow and several arrows in a quiver. He was an expert marksman with both gun and bow. I brought my .25 gun, but I don't know if Billy ever knew I had it with me. He also carried a knife and his backpack. He taught me things I didn't realize people in the twentieth century knew anything about. He had the skills to go into the fields and forests and live on what he could hunt or gather.

Every trip we took I learned something new. He showed me how to hunt and track game, how to dig a hole to sit or lay in, and to pull brush and pack dirt over you so you couldn't be seen or smelled by man or beast. He taught me how to move through the forest silently and stealthily. He taught me how to shoot a rifle with iron sights as well as a shotgun. He explained that in the wild it was important that my bullets always found their mark; that way you knew you always had something to eat. We only killed what we needed, mostly rabbits or squirrels, and he taught me how to skin and prepare wild game including fish and birds. He showed me how to keep your meat in a pot and keep the wood burning in little embers, so it wouldn't spoil. You could come back later, even the next day and have something to eat. He taught me how to build a fire and stay dry against the elements by building a lean-to. He taught me what nuts and berries that grew in the forest I could and couldn't eat. I don't know now whether it was my state of mind at that time or whether I just had an affinity for the outdoors, but I did enjoy the peace and serenity the wilderness offered.

The scenery was magnificent. We came on waterfalls, creeks flowing over rocks and springs with clear pure water. We drank the water from the springs and creeks and it was the best water I have ever tasted. In our wandering, we came across two-hundred-year-old log cabins that were still sturdy. All they needed was a bit of chinking, which had originally been done with a mixture of sand, salt, and clay. Billy also showed me ancient Indian houses built of rocks. We came across a number of ranger stations. They couldn't keep many rangers in these parts because they eventually dipped into the bootleg. Eventually, they would come down the mountain in their jeeps or trucks, run off the road, and get injured or killed.

We camped at a place Billy called Bear Cave Hollow. The cave was in a ravine near a brook, and there were large oaks and other hardwoods shading the entrance. A rather sizable old black bear lived in the cave. It was eerie; Billy seemed to have developed a relationship with the bear. It never bothered us except if we were cooking, then it would come out of the cave, sniff the air, and grunt. Billy would put sardines on a paper plate and put them on this huge rock in the middle of the brook. The bear would then come and eat them, and then walk back into the cave.

I loved Billy as a friend. I told him about my cat and he asked me to bring him along on one of our trips. I was worried about losing my cat in the woods, but Billy told me not to worry. When he met Jerry he really seemed to like him right away, and Jerry liked him. The cat went with us on the next trip; he followed us like a dog in the woods. After that, he accompanied us whenever we went hiking. If you know about cats, you know what I mean when I say I have never seen anything like it.

Between my trips to the gym and my walks with Billy, I continued to get better, but I had to get off the drugs if I was going to get strong. I finally quit them and shortly thereafter, I went through a period of clinical depression. The doctor had not told me anything about withdrawal from prescription pain pills, but it was a God-awful experience.

I was seriously depressed and worried as Tony was coming in August. Initially, it came in waves. My mood would just change for an hour or two and then it would lift again, but as it worsened, the episodes lasted longer and my thoughts became more morbid. I reflected on my life, I'd kick myself in the ass and ask, "What are you doing with your life, you stupid bitch?"

Then I'd try to talk myself out of it by concentrating on the good things I had done and the future that awaited me, but most of my episodes would wind up with me getting into my car and driving to some secluded place where I could cry without anyone hearing me. Robert Allen and I usually got together on the weekends, but I had not seen him in two weeks. When he came to pick me up at Freddy's Friday night he said, "You don't look well, Hon, are you alright?"

I remember that evening well, it was an effort for me to talk, and I was really down that night. "I-I started getting the blues a couple of weeks ago and I think it's getting worse. I just don't feel like talking or eating or fixing myself up, all I think about is how I've wasted my life and that there's no hope for you and me and Tony and anyone I care about. We're all going to die horrible deaths."

"Now Sandra, maybe you're right, given the nature of the work we're in, but you can't dwell on it or you'll go completely crazy."

"I've tried to talk myself out of it, but it doesn't do any good. Seems the more I talk to myself and point out the good things in my life, the worse I get."

"Hon, let's go out for dinner. We'll get you something to eat. You look mighty thin. Are you still working out?"

"Yes, but I don't want to eat. Freddy has been cooking all kinds of stuff trying to get me to eat, but the thought of food just makes me sick. I feel so bad I can hardly force myself to swallow. I've just been drinking water, coffee, and some soft drinks."

"How's your cat? Have you been feeding him?"

"Yes, and Freddy has been good about helping me feed him and cleaning his cat box."

"Alright, I'll give you until next weekend, but if you don't feel better then, I'm going to take you to your doctor over at St. Mary's."

"I appreciate it," I said, "I'll let you know."

I stayed to myself for the next two days, either in my room or walking in the woods. I talked to God, "If things don't get better for me soon, it's time for me to leave this Earth. There is absolutely no point whatsoever in living like this." I had lots of talks with God after that. I was headstrong and told him exactly what I liked and what I did not like in my life.

Finally, I went to see my friend Billy. I mentioned earlier that Billy Arrowood was a very spiritual man, Billy and I talked about my depression. He took me to one of the streams we visited and I guess you'd say he 'drew from the waters.' Billy had me lie down in the stream and the water flowed over my body as he chanted softly in Cherokee. Now don't scoff this off; when he was done, I felt great. I felt strong; I felt the best I had felt in my life. To this day, I cannot explain it.

******

A couple of days later, a much relieved Robert Allen came and rescued me from Freddy's. I needed a day or two to get ready for Tony's visit including telling Robert Allen and Eric Marsh that I had a plan for his visit. Tony arrived in Knoxville on August 21, a

Saturday. When he came into the airport, I didn't recognize him. I was looking for my little boy, who would turn twelve next month. Instead, a good-looking young man with long hair wearing jeans, sneakers, and a T-shirt walked over to me and looked me straight in the eye before we hugged it out.

"Good God, you're big!" I said as I held him at arm's length.

"Good God, I thought you were bigger!" He responded, proud of how he had grown in a little over six months, and his voice was changing. We both laughed.

Tony loved the car. I filled him in on Robert Allen as we stopped for lunch on our way back to the trailer. Then I asked him, "Tony, how would you like to go on a camping trip with me?"

"Sounds like fun, but what do you know about camping?"

I talked about Billy and the trips into the mountains, Tony was excited. When we got back to the trailer, I introduced my son to Robert Allen.

"He's a good looking boy, Sandra." Robert Allen said.

"You're right, mom, he does look like the Brawny man."

Robert Allen looked at me and flexed his muscles, then, we all laughed.

I stopped by Billy's on the way up to Hot Springs, North Carolina, just to let him know where I was headed and introduce him to my son. He told me about a small Ma and Pa grocery store several miles from Hot Springs that I could hike to in a couple of hours if I needed anything. We packed our backpacks and I had a double barrel 16-gauge shotgun Robert Allen lent me. Later, as we were driving east, Tony said, "Mom, you really have some cool friends."

"Cool friends, eh. Guess that was the gold standard when you're twelve." I thought.

I drove about fifteen miles into the mountains, turned onto a narrow dirt road, and parked the car in a heavy thicket. I cut down some brush and threw it on the back of the car to make its discovery more difficult. Then we began walking farther into the mountains. The further we climbed, the cooler it got as the late summer's warm air still hung heavy in the valley below.

I took Tony to some of the places Billy and I had been, the natural brooks and creeks that flowed over rocks, the magnificent overlooks, and the caves hidden by waterfalls. The most important thing about our adventure was that it gave Tony and me some one-on-one time without any disturbances. Even Jerry seemed very respectful of our time together and spent most of his time curled up in my backpack, next to the sardines. Tony caught me up on the last six months and we got to know each other again. His episodes were now once or twice a week and he told me that the doctor said they should disappear altogether in the next year as he grew. I spent my time talking to him about my friends, especially Robert Allen, and not the work. I didn't have the guts to tell my son what I was and what I was doing.

We set up camp at Bear Cave Hollow where Billy and I had camped. It was comforting to me to know that right across the stream slept a big old black bear. I always had the feeling if anything came up, like one of those large cats the mountain people call cougars, the bear would run them off. We built a lean-to and a fire ring with rocks from the stream.

We had just finished eating and were sitting around the fire talking when the bear came roaring out of the cave. The only way I can describe the noise was that it sounded like the bellow a bull makes when he puts his head down before he begins an attack. It was an awful noise.

I picked up the shotgun. "Good God Almighty, what are we going to do? I don't want to shoot the bear, but if he heads this way I'll have to."

"He wants some of what we got," Tony whispered. "I've heard stories about feeding bears in parks and then they come and want to get more and the tourists get killed." He said.

"I don't believe that bear is like that. He's fat. He has everything he wants to eat, "I said. " He's just curious and being this is his territory, if we give him some food to eat it will be like a peace offering."

 I moved over to my backpack, opened a can of sardines, and put them on a paper plate. I walked very slowly towards the rock in the brook.

"Mom! What are you doing?" I could hear the fear and panic in my son's voice.

The bear eyeballed me all the way to the rock. I put the plate on the rock and backed away to our campsite. The bear growled and shook his head, then he sniffed...then he sniffed again. Slowly, he lumbered down to the stream and into the water. He sniffed the plate a few times and then growled at us again. Tony grabbed my arm.

"Shhh..." I whispered.

The bear then sniffed the plate again and then he ate the sardines. When he was finished, he turned around and walked back to his cave, he sat down, stuck his nose in the air, took a big sniff, and then started licking his paws and his mouth. After a few minutes, he went back into the cave.

"That was so cool!" Tony shouted.

"Shhh..." Again, I whispered.

"That was so cool." Tony whispered.

"You like that, eh?"

"Yeah mom, that was really cool."

We sat up in front of the fire, Tony, me and, Jerry Crosby Miller as the woods got dark. Neither one of us really slept that night, we just stayed up talking and staring into the fire. I nodded off late.

Two days later, just after we got back from hiking, we saw the bear enter the cave with a big trout in his mouth. The next day we decided to try to find out where he was getting his fish. We walked along a number of creeks and streams, but didn't see any large trout. We returned to camp empty handed and began cooking some of the beans I had brought. Tony opened a can of sardines, emptied them onto a paper plate, and took them out to the rock. He rushed back quickly, making as little noise as possible. An hour passed and the bear did not come out to eat the sardines.

We ate dinner and talked about what we thought had happened to the bear. I thought he was in the cave and not hungry, Tony thought he was out prowling around and said he would have a tough time sleeping tonight. Just before dark, we heard a bump, bump, bump, bump coming through the forest. We turned and there he was on the other side with a big fish in his mouth.

"I'd still like to know where he's getting the fish," Tony said. "Since we're going to be here another week, we should find out. Let's just follow him in the morning."

"Not a really good idea, Tony." I said.

"Please mom, come on."

"We'll see what happens in the morning." I said

The next morning the bear left his cave. We picked up our gear and followed. We tracked him for almost two hours. Finally, we came to a posted sign, Private Property. We sneaked in anyway, and to our surprise, the property contained a trout farm. Hundreds of large trout swam in a shallow pool.

The trout farm was an easy place to get fish. All we had to do was step in knee-deep water, take a shirt, and scoop up the fish. I have never cared much for trout, but after a couple of days of eating squirrels and canned food, the fish looked really good.

That afternoon, we spied an old man hanging upside down from a tree branch over a creek. He looked about eighty years old, and he was handpicking herbs out of the edge of the water. One of the ways some mountain people made a living was by gathering wild plants and herbs to sell to pharmaceutical companies. We spoke to the old man whose name was Earl. We nicknamed him Branch Earl. He spent the afternoon showing us the various herbs and plants he was gathering, and telling us what was edible and what was not. It was a real education.

When we got back to camp, Tony and I were both hungry, so we cleaned the fish and got a fire going. The fish were great and even Jerry was happy. He liked fish better cooked than raw.

The time went by fast. Tony and I were sad when it was time to leave. We even said we would miss the bear. He had become an old friend and before we left, Tony took the hatchet, split an old log, and emptied three cans of sardines on top.

We hiked down the mountain to the car, removed the bushes, and rode down to the Ma and Pa store to get some fried chicken. Then we drove back to Robert Allen's place. He was all excited to hear about our adventure. He asked Tony to stay three more days, for the Labor Day weekend, and then took us over to Gatlinburg, Tennessee, a mountain resort town.

He had rented a two-bedroom cabin with a kitchen. The cabin sat next to a creek, partially hidden by lush vegetation. My cat loved it because we could tie him out in the shade on the creek bank and he could sit and watch the trout swim by; there may have been one or two that didn't make it.

Robert Allen was good to us. He took us out for every meal and even took us shopping at the many tourist trap stores in town. He'd drink a few beers at lunch and then was willing to walk around town with us while we spent his money. He took us to the amusement park and he and Tony rode on the rides like two kids. It made me so happy to see them getting along. Robert Allen took us to the nicest restaurants in Gatlinburg. Much of the food was not indicative of the mountains. It was Italian, Mexican, or Chinese.

After Gatlinburg, we took Tony to the airport in Knoxville. I brought the cat along to see Tony off. We went up on a balcony where you could watch the planes takeoff. On the way home, Robert Allen told me how much he enjoyed Tony's company. For the first time, in a long time, I felt happy.

Back to Work

The first week after Labor Day I met with Eric Marsh and Joseph Holt to let them know that I had contacted Codlock and was going back to work at The Court. They filled me in on the activity in Santee, South Carolina, and on The Sanctuary Hotel. The excavation was completed and the building had begun; it was scheduled to open on Saturday July 1st, the July 4th weekend of 1972. "Nine more months and I'm free," I thought.

I was living with Robert Allen, and I have to admit, I loved him. He was smart, ruggedly handsome, well built, and kind to me and my son. He loved me and made me feel safe and despite his dangerous side, I felt I could spend the rest of my life with him, but not in Newport. That very subject seemed to dominate our conversations. We wound up agreeing that we would not live in either Newport or Chicago; we would get the feds to help us relocate through their witness protection program the following year. We wanted to go to California, the San Diego area.

The first day back at The Court I walked into The Coffee Shoppe and Ted greeted me, "Sandra!" He put his big arms around me and continued, "You look great!" Then he whispered in my ear, "You did a good thing, you saved Freddy's ass, we're all real proud of you. You're quite the celebrity here now. It's good to have you back."

"Thanks Ted. It's good to be back, I missed you." I gave him a kiss on the cheek and you'd a thought he had won the lottery. His face got all red and he got very quiet as he stepped back behind his greeter's stand.

Codlock was at the counter, his second office, reading a newspaper and drinking coffee. He welcomed me back then took me inside the back room, it was dark and still smelled of incense, and we were alone.

"How are you doing, Sandra?"

"I'm well Codlock, you old bear. How are you?"

"I'm good, too, thanks. Do you have any idea of what's been happening here since you got shot?"

"No, can't say that I've been in the loop so to speak. I had a tough recovery, but the last couple of weeks have really been good for me, even been off the booze. I've been working out and hiking a lot; check out these guns." I raised my arms and flexed.

Codlock grinned, "Impressive, but we'd call those pistolas where I come from. We both laughed.

"Sandra, you're quite the celebrity around here."

"Ted said that when I came in; what's that mean, I mean what's going on?"

"There have been a ton of men come in here in the last month I've never seen before. They wanted to hook up with the prostitute that killed the hit man.

"Are you serious?"

"Absolutely! We've been telling them that you were recouping and would be back soon, but in the interim they could hook up with this girl or that girl who was a close friend of yours and they could tell them all about you. I think some of the girls have been telling some outlandish stories about you, mostly Chicago stories. The L Sisters have made a fortune this summer."

"That's great, Codlock."

"You sure were right about creating the fantasy, Sandra. See, us good old' boys can learn a new trick or two."

"I knew you could."

Things got busy at The Court that fall. While I tried to limit myself to regulars, it was impossible. It seemed that everyone wanted to bed the outlaw who killed the assassin. I made a fortune between fall of 1971 and spring of 1972, I set aside thirty thousand dollars. In December, I went home for a week at Christmas and spent time with Tony and my mom. My stepfather seemed to be under the weather, but he never told me anything when I asked him how he was feeling.

When I got back to The Court, I received a call from Harry at The Smith Truck stop in Jacksonville asking me to come down in January. I made a trip down to meet with two new pimps that had girls there. Freddy and Jerry Crosby Miller went with me; Robert Allen was away on business, moonshine business.

I met the new pimps who were moving to the Santee operation when it opened in July. Their girls were all very young including a fifteen year old that was built like a brick shit house. Freddy fell in love, and she came back with us. Vicky was a natural blonde with big blue eyes, a perfect smile, big boobs, and legs that reached to Cuba. In short, she was a Barbie doll with tits.

The Outlaw Sandra Love

She would have intimidated anyone until she opened her mouth, then she had this really sweet, naive voice like Georgette on the Mary Tyler Moore Show. Freddy paid ten thousand for her. In February, she moved in with him and he announced their engagement.

One Friday evening in late April, I was walking over to The Coffee Shoppe when I looked up and saw two cars and two pickup trucks pull into the motel parking lot. The back of each truck had a tarp over it; under the tarp were wooden cages and each cage had a rooster. I soon discovered the roosters were bred and trained in the bloody sport of cockfighting, which was then and still is illegal.

A dozen men piled out of four vehicles. They began taking turns drinking out of a jug of what I suspected and later learned was bootleg whiskey. I also found out the men, who called themselves chicken handlers, were from Harlan County, Kentucky, the home of some of the best bootleg in the country. All the men were laughing and having a good old time. Finally, one of them approached me.

"Good evening, Miss. Can you tell me if you know a young lady named Sandra Love?"

"Yes, I know Sandra." I replied.

"Do you know how I would be able to meet her?"

"Yes, I do."

"Could you tell me how I could meet her?" He asked patiently.

"Yes, first you stick your hand out like this." I stuck my hand out to shake hands. He looked at me somewhat funny and then reached out and shook my hand.

"Then I say, Hi, I'm Sandra and you are?"

"I'll be damned. You're Sandra Love aren't you?"

"In the flesh, honey."

"Well, I'm, Jim Harlan from Harlan County, Kentucky, and it is a pleasure to meet you, Sandra. All my friends call me Big Jim."

"I'm pleased to meet you, too, Big Jim."

Big Jim was around 6'4" and had hands as big as bowling balls. He wasn't fat, just big, and muscular. I found out later he was the most skilled chicken handler in the bunch. He later wrote a book, which became very popular, on breeding and training fighting roosters.

I got to be good friends with the chicken handlers. The first time I met them, they stayed the weekend. After that, they came down every weekend that spring. There were twelve men in the group and they rented three rooms. Big Jim told Codlock that they picked The Court to stay in because the men all wanted to meet the outlaw Sandra Love. They were in town for the cockfights and wanted to take me to the fights. Codlock and I talked and it was okay with me so I went to the cockfights Saturday night; so did Codlock. The handlers had their own group, a mini-Outfit that made lots of money in the cockfighting business. The cockfights were about ten miles east of Newport in the little town of Del Rio, surrounded by Great Smoky Mountain National Park. Ironically, it, like Newport, was in Cocke County.

The first time I went to the cockfights I could not believe what I was seeing. Out in the middle of nowhere was this big barn. When you went inside

187

there were bleacher seats on both sides of the ring that had at least twenty tiers of seats, and at both ends of the barn there were people standing. My guess was the barn could hold well over five hundred people. When I went in, I saw a man dressed in black about twenty yards away from me. Some big fella stepped in front of me and by the time he stepped aside, the guy in black was gone. I thought it might be Jerry Crosby Miller, but I couldn't tell.

The gamecocks, the handlers call them chickens or roosters, are bred to be powerful, fast, courageous, and to have a killer instinct. Most are brightly colored, with long spurs on their legs. The natural spurs are trimmed and artificial spurs of steel or brass put over them. The cocks use the spurs to tear and rip at their opponents and they fight until one is dead or so severely injured he can't fight.

Before each cockfight, two chicken handlers brought their birds, still in a cage, into the center of the arena. A third man entered to take bets. He chanted like an auctioneer as people in the arena raised their hands to place bets. Men in the crowd went to the person placing the bet, took his money, and gave him a slip with the number of the rooster, either one or two, on it and the amount of the bet. Bets were made in ten dollar increments so a two-thirty would mean you had thirty dollars on rooster number two. There were also hundreds of side bets in the stands. Thousands of dollars were wagered in a night...and everyone got a cut.

The times I went, there were state and local politicians, law enforcement officers and businessmen in attendance even though they all knew it was illegal. Hell, the security guys were off duty sheriff deputies that kept the crowd under control. I never did see any

TBI agents, although I know they knew about the place. It's difficult to hide a barn equivalent to the size of half a football field in a little rural community like Del Rio. Everybody knew it was there and everybody knew what was going on, but they loved it because they all made money.

I had worn a little black dress, a black shawl and heels, but no jewelry. I sat in the first row of the bleachers with Big Jim and Codlock. When Big Jim went to handle one of his roosters, a well-dressed man in black slacks, a deep burgundy mock-turtle neck jersey, and dark brown suede leather sports coat walked up and greeted Codlock. Two sheriff deputies stood behind him.

"Good evening, James Martin, nice to see you here tonight."

It was the first time I had ever heard anyone call Codlock by his given name. It was also the first time I saw Codlock move quickly. He stood up.

"Good evening your honor, how are you?"

"I'm well thanks, but I'm sure I'll be much better after you introduce me to this lovely young lady."

"This is Sandra Love. Sandra, this is Judge John McGranahan."

"It's nice to meet you, Sandra. Do you work for James Martin?"

"It's nice to meet you, too. I'm an independent contractor; I perform services for him."

"And what type of services do you perform, my dear?"

"I'm in consulting."

"Fascinating," he said with a very knowing look on his face. "What type of consulting do you perform?"

"I perform a wide range of consulting services, limited only by your imagination, your honor."

His head went back and he laughed aloud. "I'll bet you do Sandra. What area have you been consulting on with our man James Martin here?"

"We've been working on revenue enhancement, cash flow, and tax avoidance. I have also been involved with the organization's cultural change. That just about covers it doesn't it, James Martin?" I looked at Codlock.

He smiled at me and then said, "Yes, I'd say that covers it."

"Well, we've heard some good things about you Sandra. I understand you ran into a little trouble a few months ago."

"Yes...sadly, if you're going to make an omelet you're going to break an egg here and there. Wouldn't you agree?"

The Judge's demeanor changed as he turned to Codlock, "She's everything you said she was. Sandra, it was a real pleasure meeting you. I hope I'll see you again in the near future."

"It was very nice talking to you," I responded. I had remained seated and I extended my right hand.

Judge McGranahan took it, bent over, and kissed my hand.

"Oh and quite the gentleman," I said as demurely as I could.

He nodded affirmatively, shook Codlock's hand, and patted him on the back. Then he moved on, the two sheriff deputies walking a few steps behind. Codlock sat down.

"Who the hell was that?" I asked.

Codlock bent over and whispered in my ear, "That was the boss, honey, and you did great!"

"Okay, but who is he?"

"Sandra, that was Judge John McGranahan. His family has lived in Cocke County for over a hundred years. His brother Barry is the largest builder in this part of Tennessee. The two of them, along with two of their cousins, run the show here, the whole show."

"So he's kind of like the Godfather of your Outfit?"

"Yes, and honey he likes you. I've known him all my life and I know when he likes someone and when he does not. You did good, Sandra, very good. Now let's get some money on these birds."

Codlock stood up and started hollering to bet. He bet five hundred on Big Jim's rooster and won. I sat there and thought to myself, "That's it, wait until Marsh hears this!"

******

"Are you kidding me, Sandra?" Robert Allen shouted at me. It was Sunday morning and Robert Allen and I were alone in his trailer. We hadn't had much time together in the past few weeks and I was looking forward to Sunday with my man, but when I told him what had happened at the cockfights, he was just beside himself.

"Oh, Hon, you did real good. We're going to see Marsh tomorrow morning; he will shit a brick when he hears this!"

I remember that afternoon the sun was out and the temperature was in the low-seventies, nice for late March in Newport. Robert Allen and I went for a walk in the woods. We'd brought a blanket and a basket for a picnic, and I was reading this book called Love Story, a real tearjerker, and wanted to finish it. Robert Allen laughed at me as I read the end and got all emotional.

"Hon, it's a story."

"I know."

"Then why do you get so upset?"

I didn't respond at first and Robert Allen was always good at reading me, so it was quiet for a few moments. I thought about it and then I thought about whether I should answer him honestly or not. Given what I had just finished reading, I decided to share my thoughts with my love. "Maybe it's because I have to fake my emotions when I'm working. I'm so used to hiding the real Sandra, that when I let her out, she's all girlie and stuff, you know what I mean?"

"Yes, and I know the real Sandra, but I also know this, Hon," he held me in his arms as we lay side-by- side on the blanket, "in a couple of months you will never, ever have to do that again. You have my word on that."

We made love there on the blanket, off the trail on an overlook where you could see for miles; it was truly glorious. I remember how happy I was that afternoon.

Monday morning Robert Allen and I met with Eric Marsh and Joseph Holt in the Knoxville office of the FBI.

"John McGranahan. That's just unbelievable!" Marsh said. Joe Holt sat at the end of the conference table grinning like the Cheshire cat in Alice in Wonderland.

"So why can't we end this now?" Robert Allen asked.

"Codlock telling her doesn't make it true. We need evidence."

"What could Sandra possibly do to get evidence on John McGranahan?" Robert Allen was pressing Marsh.

"I think we need to go a different way here. We can get wiretaps on his phones between now and July. We can also get our Accounting Division to start looking at his tax returns and other holdings, although these people are good at hiding things. I think that you've done an outstanding job here Sandra, more than we could have hoped for, now it's just waiting for them to bring the girls up for the opening in July and then we bust the whole damn lot of them."

"We have something else to talk to you about, Eric," I said.

"What is it?"

"Please, you and Robert Allen sit down." Both of them had been pacing the room. They did. "Robert Allen and I are together. Do you understand?"

Eric leaned back in his chair, "Yes, that's great, we're happy for you guys."

"You deserve it, Sandra," Joe Holt said sincerely.

Robert Allen sat down beside me and held my hand. "Thank you," I said.

"What's on your mind, Sandra?" Eric asked.

"We want to be in the witness protection program together when this is over. We want to be relocated and we want Robert Allen's parents and my son with us. Can you do that for us?"

"Yes, and we will after you testify. Have you thought about where?"

"Yes, we'd like to live in California, San Diego County, in the mountains." I responded.

"Nice area. We can make that happen for you guys, family, too."

I felt Robert Allen squeeze my hand just a little bit. That was our deal with the feds.

I do want to share this story with you, so that you have some idea of the risk of my profession. One night in May, I had a customer who was a professional racecar driver. In all my years as a prostitute, I never liked sports people. Back at the beginning of my career, I had an experience with a member of the Chicago Bears and he almost got killed over it. He didn't even know how close he was to dying. Maybe some sports figures are appreciative of their fans, their wives and their families, but when they come to see a professional woman, they are the most outrageous, overbearing, vulgar, physically abusive, nasty, and egotistical men I have ever met. Go Bears!

At any rate, here comes this Mr. Racecar Driver and I mean he has money in his boots, money in his jacket pockets, money in his pants, and he doesn't seem to care how much he spends. He doesn't like the liquor, so he gives Codlock two-hundred dollars to go get some champagne and good whiskey. Codlock flies in his fancy car all the way from Newport to Morristown to get the champagne and whiskey and makes the trip in record time.

Now this fellow sat and talked to Linda, one of the L sisters, and me for the longest time. He said he was with me, but he liked Linda's presence. He took care of her as far as the drinks went and he kept tucking ten-dollar bills in our bras. Finally, he decided he wanted to go to a room with me. We didn't need to talk money; he'd already given me almost three hundred. When I left, I told Ted, "I'm leaving now, Ted. Hope you have a good night."

You, too, Sandra. It was code for "Keep an eye on me and this guy." Ted called Codlock.

This racecar driver, who happened to be one of the top drivers in the business, turned out to be one of the most insane people I've ever encountered. No, I will not give you his name. After the bed business, he got out of bed and whipped a pistol out of his boot, stuck it right between my eyes, laughed and said, "I think I'll kill you bitch."

He scared the shit out of me, because he was drunk and I could see how he could claim later on that his shooting me was an accident. Suddenly, Codlock began beating on the door. "Sandra, time's up. Get your ass out here now!" It was standard procedure, but there was nothing I could do with a gun pressed to my head. I tried to reason with the guy. "Put your pistol away. I'll do anything you say. You do not want to hurt me. It would ruin your career and you've got The Indianapolis 500 coming up here."

Mr. Racecar Driver got the notion that I ought to come to Indiana with him. "Oh, that's a great idea," I said. "Let me get some clothes together."

"The hell with the clothes," he said. "You go naked, just the way you are now. That's how all you whores should be all the time."

We went round and round. Finally, out of the blue, he went into the bathroom to take a leak. Boy, did I move. I went out the door bare ass naked and Codlock was there with his .38.

When Mr. Racecar Driver ran out the door, Codlock stuck his gun into his face. "Don't you fucking move!"

Then Ted grabbed his gun from behind.

"Hey, guys, we were just having some fun." He sobered up fast.

Ted and Codlock escorted him to his truck. Codlock told him, "I want five hundred for the trouble you've caused one of my girls."

The racecar driver happily gave Codlock the five hundred, crawled into his truck, and off he went. He wasn't in real good shape when he left and I never did find out if he made it to Indianapolis. Codlock split the five hundred with me.

Once in a while, I met a weirdo. Many working girls think the ones who don't do the normal straight sex or oral are weirdoes. I always thought a nice fetish added excitement and variety. I think a weirdo is someone who wants to inflict injury. He was only the second customer I met in my entire career that seriously threatened my life. However, you only need one weirdo to end up dead.

The Outlaw Sandra Love

The Sanctuary

If 1971 was a good year for whorehouses, you could safely say 1972 was a boom year. It seemed like everyone was making money. Good old supply and demand, you demand it and we supply it, but the more you demand, the higher the price. We were in the middle of a cultural revolution in the United States and thousands of service men were coming home from the war in Viet Nam every day. Sex was never so popular- thanks Hef!

On Saturday, June 24, 1972, Freddy and I packed our bags and headed down to Santee, South Carolina, a week before the hotel was set to open. We had met with Codlock to review the agenda for the opening weekend. When we got to the hotel Saturday afternoon, it was all but completed. It was beautiful.

The layout was just the opposite of The Court and included the discretion of Jacksonville's out of site thinking. The truck stop was off to the right side of the hotel. The hotel was U-shaped with a nice sized parking lot in front and a weather canopy where you could drive up and park while you went inside and registered. The lobby was full of large windows affording you a view of the front lawn where men were busy planting trees. The registration desk was on the right with offices behind it and on the left was a conference room like The Court's. In the center of the lobby were the doors that led into the restaurant. Rooms were on two floors both left and right of the main entrance, there was a set of stairs and two elevators just past the registration desk. The two wings each had thirty-six rooms, eighteen up, and eighteen down. Then there was the back building. It was another building all to itself; if you were sitting in the restaurant, you could see it out the windows and across the rear parking lot.

The Sanctuary's back building was the design that fostered the name. The syndicate had been looking for this particular enhancement. It had twenty-eight rooms and two suites...for the girls. The building had a small lobby with a reception area like a club; that's where security men would be posted. Behind that were double doors that led to a large room that could be changed to two, three, or four rooms using dividers. The room was designed for gambling, but all the hotel signs referred to the area as private meeting rooms. The difference between Santee and Jacksonville was that this building fit perfectly into the scheme of the hotel; it was hidden in plain sight. Freddy walked around with his eyes and mouth wide open.

"This is nice," He said.

I'd wager he said it a dozen times as our host, a man named Paul Johnston, showed us around the facility.

Finally, when Paul had finished the tour he asked, "Okay, what questions do you have?"

"Codlock told us you'd have a list with the dates and times the pimps are bringing the girls in. Sandra and I would like a copy and if you're available, we'd like to talk to you about room assignments," Freddy responded. "Also, is your kitchen open yet?"

"Not yet. We've been getting food and liquor in this past week. We'll start dry runs on Monday when staff is in."

"Where can we eat?" Freddy asked.

"Nowhere around here," Paul smiled. "That's the beauty of this place. Don't worry, Freddy, my first job was a cook. I'll take real good care of you and Sandra while you're here."

Paul gave Freddy the list before we had dinner. Freddy and I looked it over and talked to Paul about room assignments based on our knowledge of the girls. There were three pimps in from Jacksonville, Norman, Roy, and Freddy had girls from The Court and two pimps, Evelyn and Boo, from Mike's I-40 were also on the list. We were sitting in the kitchen eating what had to be the best fried chicken I ever tasted along with some French fries and fresh coleslaw Paul had made to go with it. Freddy turned to Paul and asked him, "Who do you have in from here?"

"Right now, there's Ed Fields and his brother Albert, Marshall Hill, and Frank Thomas."

"Damn!" Freddy said. "I know those guys from Jacksonville. That Marshall really likes to talk don't he?"

"Yea," Paul nodded, "Someday he'll brag to the wrong person."

"How many girls?" Freddy asked.

"Eight."

That gives us twenty-nine girls in twenty-eight rooms, unless you plan on using the suites?"

"No, you know who they're for, Freddy, but until Friday, I set you up in one and Sandra in the other. Two of Frank's girls are twins. They're sixteen and just came up from Georgia about three weeks ago. They'll bunk together; they work together sometimes, too...very adventurous...if you have the money."

"Paul, Freddy, and I would like to meet with them for a couple of hours. Can you arrange that?"

"It's already done, Sandra. These fellas heard all about you; I think they're more anxious to meet you than you are to meet them. We're set for Thursday night at 9pm in the back meeting room."

"That's great, that only leaves the Saturday night Grand Opening Party. I assume we'll be in that room again?" I asked.

"Yes, I understand you and a couple of other men will be speaking, Sandra."

"Tell us about security for that evening and who all will be in attendance."

Paul filled us in on the plan. The pimps and the girls were arriving Wednesday; Thursday and Friday would be orientation days. Monday afternoon I drove Freddy into Santee. He wanted to do a little shopping and eat out. While he was shopping, I went into the restaurant and phoned Eric Marsh. I told him what the plan was, the layout, and security. He planned to bust Jacksonville, Santee, Mike's I-40, and The Court all on Saturday at 9:15pm.

Paul put Freddy and I in the two suites; the suite I was in that week was sweet. The room had a huge king bed, a sitting room with a television, and a bathroom you could play baseball in.

The bathroom was all-marble, had a double sink and mirrored wall, a walk-in shower, and one of those new Jacuzzi tubs. The first night I used it I had to follow directions that were on a piece of paper in plastic that was on the side of the tub. I filled the water up until it was higher than the jets, put in a couple of squirts of bubble bath that was on the sink, and turned it on.

The jets rumbled to life and started churning the tub water.

"Eek!" It startled me when it started, but then as the bubbles started to appear I relaxed and got in. I giggled. My neck and shoulders, my thighs, and even my feet were all being massaged at once. If I wanted to change positions all I had to do was just slide the part of my body I wanted massaged up in front of one of the jets and eureka! I slid around the tub in my bubble bath relaxing and playing like a river otter, then, I got an idea...a naughty idea.

I turned sideways in the tub and put my feet up on the inside marble wall. Slowly I slid toward one of the water jets. "Oh, Oh my God! Right there...yes!" I felt my belly tense up and my legs stiffen. "This is great!" I thought, "Who needs men?" Then I thought about Robert Allen and making love in the woods, his big paw-hands gently caressing me and his body on top of mine, covering me up. As I closed my eyes, I could feel him.

The Tsunami began to build, my belly tensed, and relaxed, and then tensed again and again as it built inside me. Higher and higher, it rose as my lover, the water jets, pounded away relentlessly until...I exploded!

"Aughhhhhhhhhhh..." I moaned as wave after wave after wave of release engulfed me. My legs flopped around like two fishes as I struggled to stay in position. Suddenly, I realized it was getting hard to breathe...I choked. I opened my eyes and it wasn't Robert Allen smothering me, it was the bubbles!

I slid down the wall and then strained my neck up out of the bubbles with a big bunch of bubbles on top of my head. I looked around; I must have looked like a prairie dog peaking out of his hole. The bubbles were growing out of control, like some creature from outer space. They were climbing the walls and overflowing onto the marble floor. Suddenly I felt like I was in an episode of I Love Lucy. I reached for the button to turn off the jets, but it was covered in bubbles and I couldn't find it. Frantically, I submerged myself in the bubbles like a diver looking for treasure. Again and again, I dove under the growing mass of bubbles until I finally found the button. I turned off the jets and the room was quiet, except for that slight 'hissing' noise the bubbles made as they settled down.

Bare ass naked and wet, it took me a half-an-hour to carry the extra suds over to the shower and wash them down the drain. When I finished, I got back in the tub, turned on the jets, and just laid back and relaxed. Five minutes later, I was up to my ass in bubbles again! That was the last bubble bath I ever took in a Jacuzzi.

On Thursday night when we met with the pimps from Santee, I wore a wire.

Marshall Hill was well dressed in an expensive suit. He was of medium height and build and in his mid-forties. He had dark hair, tanned skin, and the brightest smile I had ever seen; all his teeth were capped and looked like Chiclets. Marshal was trying to break his three pack-a-day cigarette habit and was constantly chewing on a toothpick. He was from Charlotte, North Carolina.

Albert Fields was in his late fifties. He was tall and weighed around two-hundred-fifty pounds. He was in good shape for his age. His face was round and when he smiled, his eyes almost shut. He wore expensive sport clothes. He and his brother were from Akron, Ohio.

Edward Fields was a few years younger than his brother, Albert. Edward was tall and slim and had lots of gray hair tied back in a ponytail. His face was wrinkled, but he had a very nice smile. He was well-dressed, also.

Frank Thomas, in his early sixties, was the oldest and had been in the business the longest. Short and stout with broad shoulders and muscular arms, he looked like a retired wrestler. His crew cut hair was almost all gray. Born and reared in Atlanta, Georgia, he was Southern to the bone. To keep up with his fellow pimps he wore expensive clothes, but they were mismatched; he just didn't know.

Marshal started the conversation. "Sandra, I hear you've got quite a following. I wish I had you in my stable."

"If I was in your stable, you'd get all my money."

"Your pussy must be made out of gold to keep pulling in repeat customers like we hear you do," Albert said.

"It's not my pussy, it's my personality, gentlemen. My personality."

Marshal started. "I've got so many girls working for me I'm having a time keeping their schedules straight." He reached inside his suit coat, pulled out some papers, and laid them on the table. "These papers list all my girls with height, weight, hair color, measurements, age, location, and when they had their last period."

Paul and Freddy just looked at each other.

"I keep up with my girl's periods, too, "Albert said. " If you're not careful, they'll pull a fast one on you. Tell you they have to take their days off because of their monthly when I know from the schedule they had their monthly only two weeks ago. Lisa, one of my girls over in Columbia, has tried to pull that on me a couple of times. I let it go the first time, but the next time she tried to pull that trick I had to slap her around a bit. She hasn't tried it again."

By then Edward had pulled out his list of girls. "One of mine got knocked up a couple of months ago. The price you pay for an abortion is ridiculous. It eats into my profits, plus the girls are out of commission sometimes for weeks."

"Why wasn't she on birth control pills?" Paul asked. "Most of the girls are, you know."

"She was, but sometimes they just don't work," Edward said.

"Do all you guys keep detailed charts?" I asked.

"We have to," said Albert. "There's no way we could keep up with what's going on without them."

"Would you guys mind if I looked yours over before Saturday? It might help me when I talk to the girls tomorrow and with my presentation."

"Here ya go, honey, just make sure I get it back before I leave next week." Marshall tried to hand me his, but I played dumb.

"Do me a favor; just put your name on each so I don't screw it up."

All of them pulled out their gold Cross pens and wrote their names on the documentary evidence. When I reviewed the lists, there were twenty-three girls out of thirty-six that were under eighteen. Four of them were at The Sanctuary for the opening.

Friday, I met with the girls. I asked for them in two groups. I met with the older girls for breakfast and I met with the underage girls for lunch. Paul had his staff in and working; again, I was wearing a wire. I got the conversation rolling. "I'm from Chicago. Where you ladies from""

"I'm from Atlanta, "Brenda Sue said in her heavy southern drawl.

I'd been in the South long enough to feign an accent, so I just said, "Why, I declare."

"I'm from Jacksonville," Kathy said.

"I was in Jacksonville last year," I told her.

"I heard you used to be a pimp," Jeanie said.

I looked at her. "Oh, I've done lots of things. Where are you girls from?"

Jeanie and Jenny were the twins, "We're from Savannah."

"Savannah. Love the river walk shops."

Jenny looked at me. "How'd you get in this business?"

I told her the truth. "My son had a lot of medical problems and I wasn't making enough money as a cocktail waitress. So, when a customer told me I could make more money as a working girl, I decided to do it. He helped me get a job at a hotel in Gary, Indiana."

"How could you make good money?" asked Jeanie. "You must not have had a pimp."

"I didn't. I worked for The Outfit, or as you know them, the Mafia. I freelanced, five hundred a trick.

"You're her!" Jenny said. You killed a hit man in Tennessee didn't you?"

"Yes, I did."

"Why aren't you in jail?" Jeanie asked. The twins were tag teaming me.

"Self defense, honey. Now, do you ladies know why I'm here?

"I hope it ain't to teach us how to screw, we already know that!" Jenny said.

"And the rest" Jeanie said and then pressed her tongue into her cheek so that her cheek bulged out. I laughed out loud, and then the whole group laughed. It was an icebreaker.

"I'm here for one reason only, to help you make more money."

We talked about customer service and creating the fantasy. The girls asked a lot of questions. I told them I planned to be there for the first month and that we would meet again after I talked with their pimps. They were all excited, even the twins. I got back to my suite and opened up a bottle of Vodka I bought while I was in Santee. If everything went all right, this would be my last night in this business and I could start my new life. I spent that night toasting my new life and remembering why I was here...my Tony. I missed him, I loved him; I drank myself to sleep.

In the morning, around 9:15am, someone pounded on my door. "Let's go, Princess, rise and shine. It's moving day."

I let Freddy in. He spotted the bottle, "You okay?"

"Missed my son last night. When this is over Freddy I'm going home."

"Forever?"

"We'll see," I said. "We'll see."

Paul had moved us to regular rooms upstairs in the back of the front building. It gave me a perfect view of the back parking lot. I spent the morning checking on all the little details that go into having an event like the Grand Opening party. By early afternoon, everything was ready and all the staff were in and working. In the lobby, folks were already checking in. Paul had a huge white temporary sign out in front that announced the opening on July 1st. It was exciting to watch and it got more exciting around 4:30pm.

The phone rang in my room. "Hello."

"Sandra, this is Paul. Codlock is here and he has some players with him. He wants you and Freddy down here now. They're in the front conference room."

"Did you call Freddy?"

"Not yet."

"I'll get him."

I pulled my hair back in a ponytail, slipped into a black mini-skirt, white blouse, and heels, put on fresh lipstick and picked up Freddy on the way downstairs since his room was next to mine.

John McGranahan, his brother Barry, and two cousins, Floyd and Gerald Yocum, were waiting for us with Codlock in the conference room off the main lobby. Two large men stood in front of the doors. Paul escorted Freddy and me through the gauntlets.

"Sandra!" Codlock shouted and walked across the room from the table where they were sitting and hugged me. "Are we ready?" He whispered as the other men stood up, southern gentlemen style.

"Yes, relax. This is going to be an exciting evening."

"Paul, Freddy, come on over here. There are introductions needed." Codlock waved at the two.

We were all introduced to each other and we spent the next couple of hours talking about the facility. At first, I thought I'd made a mistake by not wearing a wire, but the Judge never really said anything that would indicate he was the boss of the syndicate. He just asked a lot of questions about the facility and the girls. Paul fielded most of the facility questions. Freddy and I answered questions about the pimps and the girls, and Codlock talked about rates, splits and other revenue issues like gambling. Floyd took lots of notes as we were talking.

Around 6:45pm I said, "If you gentlemen will please excuse me I'm going up to my room and make myself all pretty for our party tonight. Dinner is at eight and then speakers at nine."

"Just a minute Sandra, before you go," Judge McGranahan said, "We are all appreciative of what you and Freddy have done for us this past year, particularly with that mess you had last spring. We might not be quite as big as the folks you know in Chicago, but we do know how to say thank you. We'd like to show our appreciation, James Martin."

As Codlock reached into his jacket pocket, I saw his gun and shoulder holster. He handed me an envelope full of money and then gave another to Freddy.

"Thank you, John," I said, "glad we could help." Freddy nodded.

"Why don't you thank me tonight at 10pm in my room? I believe it's the suite you stayed in this week."

"Absolutely," I smiled.

Barry McGranahan turned to Paul saying, "Floyd and Gerald like to shop for themselves, but I'd appreciate it if you can get those twins up to my suite at ten."

"Done," Paul, responded.

Freddy and I went to our rooms. Each envelope had five thousand dollars inside. I struggled with Judas feelings as I bathed, dressed, and packed my bags.

At 8pm, I was dressed and looking out my window at the rear parking lot; nothing. I saw no vans, panel trucks, or even cars with men, and no sign of the feds. I hadn't seen or heard from Eric Marsh since my phone call to him on Monday. I left for dinner.

Paul had brought in special food and drink for the event. He offered any top shelf liquor you wanted, shrimp cocktails, filet mignon with mushrooms, potatoes, or grits, and steamed garden beans followed by crème Brule and coffee or tea. There were thirty-one women and twenty men in the room when Paul stood up at a podium and began speaking. He welcomed his 'partners' and thanked everyone for coming. He said he wasn't much for public speaking, but...

Suddenly, the double doors behind us burst open and in came the feds, all thirty-five of them dressed in flak jackets that had FBI in big large letters. I heard a familiar voice.

"Federal agents! We're the FBI; don't anyone in this room move. Put your hands on top of your heads now!"

No one moved, confused by the conflicting statements, as dozens of agents poured into the room holding semi-automatic handguns.

"Put your hands on top of your heads, NOW!" Eric shouted as the agents spread out around the room and encircled the seven tables.

I put my hands up on top of my head and everyone else at my table followed suit. Those at the other tables followed the drill, except Judge McGranahan who shouted out to Marsh, "Are you arresting these people, officer? On what charge? Do you know who I..."

"Yes, we are! Variable charges your honor!" Yes, I know who you are. You're the head of a syndicate who's been trafficking underage women across state lines for the purpose of prostitution." Two agents grabbed the judge and began to cuff him as Marsh continued, "You are in violation of US Code Title 18,

Chapter 77. Then, we have several hundred counts of Exploitation of Minors, kidnapping, violations of Civil Rights, extortion, murder, illegal transportation and selling of firearms, various violations of the RICO Act...and my personal favorite, Income Tax Evasion. You've been a bad boy your honor!"

"Prove it!" McGranahan shouted as the FBI cuffed him.

"Here, in Jacksonville or Newport...no problem. Take this guy out of here!"

Some of the girls in the room began crying as their pimps were cuffed and taken away. I saw Paul, Codlock, and Freddy cuffed and removed before Joe Holt came over to me and said, "Stand up Miss and put your hands behind your back."

"Not until you put two hundred dollars on the table you son-of-a-bitch!" Holt forced me down on the table and cuffed me as the twins started hollering.

"Kick him in the nuts, Sandra!" Jenny shouted.

"You can blindfold me for a hundred! Jeanie hollered as she was handcuffed, too.

Holt took me out past the two security guards who sat handcuffed on the floor, but when we got outside, he lead me over to a black car and put me in the backseat. Another agent was in the driver's seat. Then, Joe un-cuffed me."I have a bag in my room and my purse; here's the key." I reached down into my bra, pulled out the key to my room, and gave it to Holt. "It's Room 200. Please bring me my purse."

"Bill, go get it."

The agent in the driver's seat left and came back in a few minutes putting my suitcase in the trunk and handed me my purse. Joe Holt and I talked for about a half an hour before the passenger side front door opened and Eric Marsh got in.

He turned around. "It's over! We got the bastards in Jacksonville, Newport, and the I-40 operation, all without a hitch."

"Here's some gravy for your potatoes, Eric." I handed him the wire I had worn and the pimp's schedules. I explained what they were and told him, "I even got them to autograph them for you."

Marsh looked at the papers as we drove, "You're incredible."

The agents were happy. I was happy, too, but for an entirely different reason. I was going home. "What now?"

"We're taking you over to Columbia, Sandra. I have some bad news for you."

"What, what is it Eric?"

"Your stepfather had a heart attack on Tuesday and died. Your mother called our office; she has been trying to reach you for the last three days. We're flying you home on a private plane out of Columbia tonight."

Live by the Sword

"Sandra!" My mom gasped as she opened the front door of her house. We hugged on her front porch as she cried. The agent that drove me home set my bag and purse down and left quietly; it was almost 2am.

"Mom, I'm home, it's going to be alright." After a minute, we went inside and I made some coffee. My mom was clearly shaken.

"Where have you been? I called the FBI office and they wouldn't tell me anything except you'd be in touch."

I told my mom about what had happened, that my adventure was over, and that I would be home for a while and then Robert Allen and his parents and Tony and I would be relocating under the witness protection program. I told her she could come, too.

"Oh Sandra, my life has just been turned upside down. I don't know what I'm going to do without Joe. Tony is upstairs sleeping; Mrs. Lewis brought him over on Wednesday. He's been such a great help. It's like my head is spinning; I-I can't think straight. I-I was so worried about you. I thought they were lying to me. I thought you were dead."

"Mom, everything is going to be alright. I'm home now." I held my mother's hand and we sat in the kitchen until 4am talking. She told me the funeral services were on Monday. "Let's get some sleep and we'll sort everything out in the morning," I said. Mom and I slept together that night. She felt smaller than I remembered as we cuddled together; she had lost some weight I guessed, then I fell off to sleep.

"Good morning."

I opened my eyes and there stood Tony bending over the bed and shaking my shoulder.

"Shhh," I whispered and then got out of bed. We hugged and then we went out to the kitchen and I fixed him Sunday breakfast: scrambled eggs, pancakes, and sausage. It was around 11am. I explained that I would be leaving my job with the FBI in Tennessee and we would be moving to the west coast with Robert Allen and my mom if she decided to go. I braced myself for the normal teenage reaction, 'Mom, what about my friends here?' It never came.

"Will you still be with the FBI, mom?" Tony asked.

"No, honey, that's over."

"What will you be doing?"

"Why do you ask, Tony?"

"I don't want you to take another job that means you'll be away again."

"Oh, honey," I said, "not again, I promise."

My mom came out around noon and only drank coffee. She was very quiet. I had gone through a bout of depression after I was shot, so I recognized her behavior and could relate. Tony and I left her alone for most of the day.

Monday was my stepfather's funeral; over a hundred and fifty friends and relatives attended. I had an opportunity to talk with Mrs. Lewis so I thanked her for her help with Tony over the past two years and told her he would be staying with us now. She thanked me over and over again for the money I had sent her; she said it was a Godsend. Then I saw someone that I had not seen in ten years. It was Grayson...my first customer and friend from the hotel in Gary.

"Hi, Sandra."

"Hi, Sandra? That's it?" I wrapped my arms around him and gave him a big hug, and then I kissed him on the lips and smiled.

He shook his head and said, "You always were a bit bull headed." We went outside to talk about the 'old days' and I thanked him for being so kind to such a young girl. We talked and caught up on our lives. I told him about Newport. He told me he had heard rumors about me out there. Then he got serious.

"Sandra, you don't want to be here if they put a hit out on you. If they know you're from Chicago, they'll track you down and kill you before you can testify. Get in the witness protection program as soon as possible. If you need any help, we can call Jackie Kramer."

I thanked him for his advice. It was the last time I ever saw anyone from The Outfit. When I got home, I called Robert Allen to find out what was going on in Newport, but there was no answer.

Tuesday was the 4th of July. I spent most of the day helping my mom with financials. Joe had a twenty-five thousand dollar life insurance policy, the house was mortgage free, and her car was paid off. I went through her checkbook and put a monthly budget together for her in case she decided to stay. That night I called Robert Allen again, still no answer. Wednesday morning Tony went to play baseball and my mom was still in bed. Around 11am, I called Robert Allen again, when there was no answer I decided to check in with his parents.

Robert Allen's mother answered, "Hello."

"Hi Rebecca, it's Sandra. I've been trying to reach Robert Allen for the last couple of days. Have you seen him?"

"Oh, Sandra," she started to cry, "They shot him in The Smokey Mountain Club Monday night. He's dead."

"Whaaa...NOOOOOOOOOOOOOOOOOOOOOO...OH GOD... NO! NO! NO! NO! NO!"

I slammed the phone down on the edge of the table as I screamed no again and again, "Oh God, please don't do this to me...please...please...please..." I wailed as I cried for a couple of minutes then I heard Rebecca on the line.

"Sandra...Sandra...listen to me...Sandra...please... honey...Sandra can you hear me?"

"Oh God, Rebecca...OH GOD, REBECCA! I broke down crying and sobbing again. I had never cried that hard in my whole life and to this day, I never have again. My love was gone. My love was dead!

Then just as I thought the pain was going to kill me, I felt two arms around my neck and shoulders; my mother was up.

I dropped the phone, and turned and cried in my mother's arms for a few minutes as she held me.

Finally, I blurted out, "They shot him, those bastards killed Robert Allen."

My mother pushed me away and held me at arm's length, "Who shot him?" She asked.

"I- I don't...where's the..." I grabbed the phone off the floor, "Rebecca? Rebecca, are you still there?" I shouted as I wiped away the tears.

"Yes, I'm here."

"Who shot him Rebecca, do you know?

"Joel Cole shot him over at The Smokey Mountain Club...and Mike McCleod was there, too. Listen to me Sandra, do not come back here, they're on to you. Everybody in town is talking about you since Saturday night when the FBI closed down The Court." Rebecca's voice quivered as she spoke.

"When's the funeral?"

"Today at 4pm. There wasn't any viewing; they shot him in the head. MY BOY..." Rebecca broke down crying and then Melvin, Robert Allen's dad, came on the line.

"Sandra, this is Mel."

"What's it like there, Melvin?"

"I heard there are some people that are really mad at you, but there's also some that think you're a hero. They said you were an undercover FBI agent all this time, but after Robert Allen was killed they ain't talking much now, too scared. Don't come down for the funeral, they're waiting for you, honey."

"Thanks, Melvin, you take real good care and I'll see you again someday. Melvin, I loved your son very much."

"And he loved you, Sandra. Take care."

I hung up. I walked over to the liquor cabinet and pulled out a half a bottle of vodka.

My mother turned to me. "Please Sandra, don't..."

I took a long, long drink of vodka. My mom and I talked as I drank. After a while, I called the FBI office in Knoxville. Emma answered.

"Emma, this is Sandra. I need to talk to Eric now!"

"Good morning, Sandra. Can you give me your ID number?"

"Emma, I've been calling you every week for two years. Do you really still need my ID?" I took another swig of vodka as I watched my mother sit down and shake her head. I remember thinking, "Everyone is so fucking judgmental."

"Yes, Sandra," Emma replied in that cheery professional business voice she had, "I need your ID number."

I took another swig and now I had a quarter of a bottle of vodka in my hand. "Well, if you just bend over and wait awhile, I'll drive down there and shove my ID number up your ass. Now put him on the line," I screamed as I felt the tears welling up in my eyes. I guess looking back on it now, Emma could feel my distress through the phone.

"One moment."

I waited and drank and waited. Finally, Eric Marsh came on the line.

"This is Agent Marsh."

I blew. "Don't give me that Agent Marsh shit Eric, Robert Allen is dead! Didn't you have the guts to call me?"

"Sandra, I'm sorry. We didn't find out until last night...it was the holiday...and with your mom's loss, I was going to call you this morning. How are you doing?"

"How do you think I'm doing, Eric, my man is dead! What are you guys doing about it?"

"Sandra, you know how it is there. If we can get just one witness who will testify, but it's a damn culture in Newport...you don't rat!"

"That's it? If you think for a minute that I'm going to stand by while someone kills my man and do nothing about it, you don't know a thing about me."

"Sandra, don't do anything stupid. You could jeopardize..."

"No Eric, nothing stupid. I'll call you." I hung up.

My mother sat on the couch wringing her hands. I never saw her that distraught before.

"Sandra, please don't..."

"Mother, please don't tell me what to do, you don't know anything about this."

"Well, I know if you live by the sword you die by the sword. Is that how you want to live your..."

"What are you saying mother, Robert Allen deserved to die?"

"No Sandra, I'm just worried about..."

"Stop worrying about me, mom. I can take care of myself."

"You're not listening to me, Sandra. You need to think of Tony and..."

The liquor was starting to get to me. I was hurt, angry, and frustrated. My whole future had been destroyed in a moment and my mother, who I had been caring after for the last few days, was trying to give me advice about something that she knew nothing about. I wheeled around and all the pain and horror of the last two years of my life exploded out of me fused by the vodka.

"Think of Tony? He is all I've ever thought about for the last thirteen years! Forgive me, mother, if I was thinking about myself for a moment when I found out those bastards shot my love in the head. Don't you think I was thinking about Tony when I was a prostitute in Gary...or a call girl for The Outfit...or a truck stop whore in Tennessee? Do you know what I've done for Tony, mother? Do you know about the filthy pigs I've slept with, the men whose dicks I've sucked, and the perverts that played their twisted little games with me like I was their personal sex slave? How about the lies I've told, the people I've betrayed, and the young women that I tried to help...can I think about any of them for just a minute without you telling me to think about Tony! I've been shot; I've killed a man...what if I want to think about them mother...WHAT IF I WANT TO THINK ABOUT ME!"

Live By The Sword

I was hysterical, ranting at my mom in a way I had never done before. I looked down at her; her eyes were transfixed with horror and fear. It was then I noticed she wasn't looking at me. She was looking behind me. I turned around...there stood Tony, his bat over his shoulder and his glove hanging from it.

Every ounce of fear my mother felt instantly transferred to me as I saw the look on his face and the tears running down his cheeks.

"T-Tony...I-I..." I couldn't think of anything to say.

Tony turned and ran for the door. I ran after him, but I was drunk and he was thirteen; it was no contest. In an instant, he was gone as I screamed, "TONY!" and collapsed sobbing on the floor. I cried and cried as my mom came over and sat down beside me. My head fell into her lap and she stroked my hair as I cried.

Several hours later, I had showered and sobered up a bit. I packed my bag and after I apologized to my mom, we talked about the future. Tony was to stay with her until I got home. It would be better if she was not alone in that neighborhood and the FBI money was going to stop after I testified. She would try to fix the damage I had done. I called Mrs. Lewis to let her know that I would be by to pick up my Firebird. My mom drove me over to Gary and after what was a tearful good bye I left in the Firebird on my way to Newport. I had but one thought, "Someone's going to die...and soon."

******

I drove for about three hours before I pulled into a motel for an overnight in Indianapolis, Indiana. I got a coffee and a carton of cigarettes at a convenience store next to the motel. I needed some time to think through what I was going to do. I had a bag full of clothes, my car, my gun, and almost five thousand dollars. I went to bed around 9pm. I woke up at 8am Thursday morning feeling rested.

I needed a day and I took it. Behind the motel was a creek and I went and sat down along the bank for a few hours. I needed to get my arms around this mess. It was a nice sunny day, the temperature was in the mid-eighties, and I had a lot to think about.

I spent the day in reflection down by the creek. I cried, I laughed, and I prayed for Robert Allen. I talked to God. I made my peace and then I got strong. I spent the night at the hotel and Friday when I woke, I did my rehab exercises, pushups, sit-ups and then went for a mile run. When I got back, I showered and dressed in jeans, sneakers, and a tank top. I wore some dark sunglasses and a ball cap. I checked out, grabbed a coffee and some sandwiches, and left for Newport. I got in around 2pm.

I drove around town, but did not go near The Court. I drove up into the mountains to the overlook where Robert Allen and I had made love that afternoon in the woods. I lay down on the ground where we had been. I couldn't help myself; I got teary again. I kissed the ground and swore an oath. I lay there and watched as the sun went down. I felt strange. Many different thoughts raced through my mind: Tony and my mom, Robert Allen, Eric Marsh, Freddy and Codlock, my life, but my brain kept returning to one thought...Joel Cole and Mike McCleod.

At 9pm, I drove over to The Smokey Mountain Club. There were a lot of trucks and cars in the parking lot. I drove by and went up the mountain to a dirt road that was a fire trail for the rangers. I parked my car and walked down through the woods until I could see The Rocky Mountain Club. I sat on a log and waited. The woods aren't dark at night; they are black. You can hear many sounds, mostly deer out browsing, but I had my gun and an extra clip with me just in case. A little after midnight, the lot started to thin out. Men were coming outside, some to go home, some to fight..."beer muscles," I thought.

By 2am there were only two trucks left in the lot. I made my way back to the car and drove to the road. As I got to the club, I killed the engine and the lights and coasted down into the far end of the parking lot. I got out of the car and crept to the front window, my gun in hand. I looked inside; there was no sign of anyone. I went over to the other window that looked in on the poolroom; Joel Cole and Mike McCleod were playing pool and drinking beer.

I went back to the front door and tried to open it. It opened. "Morons," I thought.

I could hear the sounds of the balls clicking and I could hear them talking and laughing. The TV was on in the bar so I could move without them hearing me. I crept over to the doorway and then stepped out, my gun up. Both men had their back turned to me. Joel bent over the table; he shot and pocketed a ball.

"Nice shot, shithead!"

The two of them turned and saw me; their eyes got big.

"S-Sandra...what are you doing, girl?" Mike McCleod sputtered out.

"You shouldn't have shot Robert Allen, you little bastard!" I screamed.

"I didn't shoot him, Joel did!" He pointed at Joel.

"Both of you put your hands on top of your heads, real slow, now!"

They dropped the pool sticks and put their hands on top of their heads.

"When you're ready to die, move your hands and I will shoot you dead!"

The two froze.

"Why did you kill my love, asshole?" I pointed the gun at Joel.

"Sandra, he was working for the feds, it wasn't personal, just business."

"Yep, well, don't take this personal, Joel." I raised the gun sight from his heart to right between his eyes. Then..."CLICK."

I heard the hammer of the gun behind me cock, then I felt the gun barrel against the back of my head and heard a familiar voice, "Don't you fucking move bitch or I'll blow your brains out!"

A hand appeared over my left shoulder, "Gimme."

In an instant I thought, "Why didn't you shoot, Sandra? Robert Allen told you, 'If you point, you shoot.'" My hands lowered a bit and then the man behind me grabbed the gun.

"Hello, Sandra." The man stepped around in front of me; it was Norman.

"Forgive me for not joining your party, earlier. I had to drain the monster." His fat, ugly face smiled and I think I actually shivered. "Now, however, I'm ready to party with the whore from Chicago."

"Shoot me, you pig, I'd rather be dead."

"Oh, you're going to die alright, but it's going to take a lot longer than you ever could imagine."

"Fuck you!"

Norman swung his gun and pistol-whipped me. The gun caught me on the temple and I went down.

My head spun and I heard voices shouting. I felt them pick me up and then someone tore off my top and bra and started grabbing and squeezing my breasts really hard. I felt my jeans being pulled down and then felt Norman slapping my face.

"Come on, tough girl, snap out of it. I want you to feel everything that's going to happen to you now."

I opened my eyes; Joel and Mike had my arms pulled over my head and my jeans and panties were down around my ankles. I lay stretched out on the pool table with my butt propped up on the rail and Norman was standing between my legs with his fly down. He grabbed my nipples with his two hands and twisted them hard.

"You bastard, do it and get it over with."

"I'll do what I want to you, when I want to," The pig yelled at me, then spit in my face.

"Yeah, Dixie, fuck her," Joel hollered.

"Ride her hard, Dixie." Mike was egging him on too.

I felt him slide inside me then he started banging away as hard as he could as he grabbed my breasts and squeezed hard, then, he started yanking them around. The pig just wanted to hurt me. "This was going to be my one too many weirdoes," I thought.

Norman raped me. He slapped me around a good bit and finally climaxed. I looked up at his fat, sweaty face; he was panting and smiling. "Don't know what's so good about your pussy, seemed like all the other pussy I've had." Norman sneered.

I turned my head and closed my eyes.

"Let's shoot her up for a few days and have some fun with her, then take her up to Jesse's and let those moonshine boys keep her as a pet. I heard they know just how to treat a slut like her," Mike laughed.

"I heard that old son of a bitch kept a whore chained to a tree like a dog for ten months before she died of pneumonia," Joel grinned.

"This bitch isn't going anywhere until I have my fun with her," Norman said as he pulled out of me, reached into his pants pocket, and opened up a switchblade knife. "I heard in some countries that if a woman sleeps around a lot, they cut off her button. Let's take a closer look at yours, bitch." Norman lowered the knife until it was between my legs. I looked back up at his fat pig face and his evil grin as he looked down on me. Then Norman's face exploded.

It sounded like a stick of dynamite went off in the room. Norman's face disappeared as blood and brains splattered all over me, and the pool table. His body fell on top of me then slid down my belly smearing blood all over me before he fell to the floor.

I heard a voice say, "Let her go now!"

Joel and Mike let go of my wrists and I turned sideways and pushed myself up, then I wiped some of Norman's brains off my face. I looked up, and standing in the doorway of the poolroom, was my black knight, Jerry Crosby Miller, his .357 magnum still smoking.

I pulled my panties and jeans up, pulled my bra down, and took off my ripped top. I bent over the corpse that was Norman Dixon and pulled my pistol out of his pants waistband. I turned toward the two men. I raised my pistol and aimed it at Joel's head, then, I walked forward. I got about three feet from his head; his eyes were as big as saucers. Then I spoke, "Thou shall not kill." I pulled the trigger.

A small hole appeared in the middle of Joel's forehead and then blood ran out as he pitched to his right and fell over. I held the gun a foot from the back of his head and pulled the trigger again. His head moved slightly from the impact and Joel Cole lay still. I walked around the end of the pool table, my gun aimed at Mike's head.

"Please, Sandra, don't kill me." He fell to his knees and begged for his life.

I walked up to him, my gun a foot from his face. "Robert Allen sends his regards." I pulled the trigger. Mike's pleading stopped immediately as his body dropped backwards and to the right. The room was silent. I stood over his body and aimed at the side of Mike's head, my gun six inches from his temple. I pulled the trigger, again. I lowered the gun and turned to Jerry Crosby Miller, "Two in the head, is that how it's done?"

"Yes, that will do it." He responded very calmly.

As I started to walk towards him, my legs began wobbling and just before I collapsed, he holstered his gun, grabbed me under the arms, took my gun from my hand and then he helped me into a booth in the main bar room. I sat down while he got me a clean bar towel filled with ice for my head, then he brought me a drink of water.

"How do you feel?" He asked.

"That pig raped me, squeezed my breasts so hard they'll be black and blue for a month and was going to cut off my...how the hell did you find me?" I took a sip. "What is this crap, water?"

Jerry sat down. He had a glass with ice and a soda. He took his time responding as he poured the soda into the glass, "Never drink on the job Sandra, it doesn't pay." He pushed the soda towards me. I picked it up and drank some. After a few moments he said, "We've been following you since you hit town this afternoon. Mel called me after he talked to you. He said he thought you'd show up soon."

"I wonder how that old fart knew what I was going to do."

"He said it was pretty easy to figure. He said he warned you not to."

"You said we, who's we?" I asked.

Live By The Sword

Jerry lit a cigarette and pointed past me towards the front door, "Me, and my chauffer."

I turned around and there stood my Jake.

He ran over as I slowly slipped out of the booth. He stopped a couple of steps short, reached out with both arms and we embraced. He held me in his arms for a few minutes and then whispered softly, "You okay?"

"I'm tired." I looked up at that beautiful face and put my hand up on his cheek. "Thanks."

"No worries."

"Sandra, if you have the keys to your car, Jake will take you over to Billy's. I'll be about a half an hour behind you."

I gave Jerry the keys and Jake and I left; his cab was down the road past my car. When we reached the bottom of the mountain, Jake pulled over and said, "Look at that."

I leaned across the front seat and looked out the driver's window. Halfway up the mountain you could see the orange and red glow of The Smokey Mountain Club as it burned to the ground.

Parting With The FBI

It was past 4am in the morning when Jake and I pulled up in front of Billy Arrowood's cabin. Billy sat on the front porch in a rocking chair with something in his lap; I assumed it was a gun. When we stopped and Jake turned off the cab's lights, Billy stood and as I got out of the cab, he approached me carrying Jerry Crosby Miller, my cat, in his arms.

"Jerry!" I shouted as I rushed forward, but I could see right away he wanted nothing to do with me.

"Give him time, Sandra; time is the greatest healer we have." Billy said in his deep, soft voice.

"Okay, I will."

Billy looked at my bruised and battered face, "Come inside, we need to take care of you now." Billy held the cat as Jake and I followed him into the cabin. The cabin had a sitting area with a sofa, chair, and coffee table that sat in front of a fireplace. Off to the left was the kitchen with a small round kitchen table and four chairs; the cabin had two back bedrooms. An outhouse and a freestanding garage were outside. Billy tended to my face as I sat at the kitchen table. Jake stood by the window watching nervously.

When Billy was through, I went outside to the outhouse taking a wet cloth with me. I took off my jeans and then ripped my panties off and threw them down the hole. I would not have them touching me ever again; they were dirty with that pig Norman. I cleaned myself up and went back to the cabin. Billy had fixed coffee, and he gave me a cotton shirt to wear. The three of us sat, had coffee, and smoked while we filled Billy in on what had happened. Then I felt Jerry Crosby Miller rub against my legs. I looked down and he jumped up into my lap and started purring. I looked at Billy, "Time."

He smiled at me and said, "Your other Jerry is here."

There was a knock on the screen door, "Hello." It was my black knight, Jerry Crosby Miller.

"Come in," Billy called.

Jerry came in.

Jake turned to Billy and asked, "How is it you heard him coming?"

"How is it you didn't?" Billy replied.

Jake smiled, "Everything okay?"

"All cleaned," Jerry, told us.

"Coffee?" Billy asked as he stood and walked towards the stove.

"Yes, thanks." Jerry walked over to me and put his hand on my shoulder, "How are you?"

"I'm fine, thanks to my friends."

The sun was starting to rise as Jerry Crosby Miller and my Jake left Billy's cabin. We had talked about the last two years, why I was there and where I was going now. I thanked them for what they had done and for being such good friends. Jerry kissed my hand in true black knight fashion. My Jake took a bit longer, "I guess you know how I feel about you."

"Yes..."

"Will I ever see you again?"

"I just don't know, but maybe."

He hugged me and then said, "You were a hell of a woman before tonight, but now that I know why you were here and what you've done, I've got to tell you, you're the best woman I've ever known."

"Be well." I said.

"You, too, Sandra."

Jerry drove my Firebird and Jake followed him in his cab. They took my car and luggage to Robert Allen's garage and hid it there. I stood on the path and waved goodbye to my friends; I never saw either one of them again. I was so sad.

Billy had a bed for me back in the guest room. I fell asleep with Jerry Crosby Miller purring by my side. I slept until noon. When I awoke, Billy fixed lunch and we talked for a while. He planned to drive me to Knoxville Monday morning in his truck to meet with Eric Marsh. I spent Saturday and Sunday walking in the woods with Billy. These days were some of the more peaceful days I'd spent in Newport. It was the beginning of a transition period for me; I just didn't know it at the time.

At 2pm Monday afternoon, I walked into the Knoxville office of the FBI. Emma escorted me to a conference room.

After a short wait, Eric came in carrying a few files with him. He looked at my face as he sat down across the conference table from me, "Looks like you took some incoming Friday night."

"I held my own."

"I'll say. They found the remains of three bodies. They are doing the ID checks now. Do you want to tell me, so we can talk intelligently?"

"I heard Joel Cole, Mike McCleod, and Norman Dixon left town last week; you won't be seeing them around anymore."

"Sandra, what have you done?"

"Do you read the Bible, Eric? It says, "An eye for an eye."

"The part I read was, 'Vengeance is mine,' said the Lord."

"Consider me the Lord's messenger."

"Is that the name you are going to use when you testify? 'I, the Lord's messenger, do solemnly swear to tell the truth, the whole truth and nothing but the truth so help me God.' Because if it is, we'll have a bigger problem than we have now."

"What problem?"

"Sandra, you killed three men! How the hell are we going to put you on the witness stand?"

"How is that related to what I'm going to testify about?"

"Norman Dixon, Mike McCleod, and Joel Cole, two pimps and the man who shot Robert Allen. Sandra, it's your credibility that would be targeted, not in direct, but in cross. And, this isn't the first time; you killed that hit man last year. We'll have enough difficulty with your background in The Outfit and what you did undercover, but this...this opens up a new door for their attorneys."

"Eric, I was with The Outfit for more than four years, don't try to bullshit me. You people would have rats lined up three deep if they were going to bag you a bust you could make stick and those guys were all felons. You knew what I would be doing undercover from the beginning. So what is this crap you're giving me now? Why are we talking about this, instead of when me, my mom, and Tony are leaving for California?"

"Freddy agreed to turn this morning, if we gave him full immunity."

"Great, now you've got two rats!"

"He hasn't killed four men."

"Neither have I, someone else got Norman before I could and no one can prove I killed Joel and Mike. It's not what you think; it's what you can prove. Now spit out whatever you have to say to me after two years."

"You might not like this, Sandra, but right now we've got you by the short ones, not the other way around."

"Maybe I didn't always do things your way, Eric, but I'm alive and you got what you were after. Now it's time to pay the piper!"

"Maybe the piper ought to stop blowing her own horn and start doing what's right."

"Maybe the piper didn't kill all the rats!"

"Are you threatening me, Sandra?"

"If the shoe fits, Eric?"

"Damn woman! You're something else."

"Brace yourself Agent Marsh, there's more coming behind me."

He seemed to stop and think about that for a long minute then, "You may be right, with all this women's lib shit." Eric pushed his chair back from the table and stood up; he was still pissed. He walked to the end of the table and then back. He took a deep breath, reached in his pocket, and pulled out a box of Marlboro's, "Cigarette?"

"Thank you."

He leaned across the table and lit the cigarette for me, then, he lit one for himself and sat down.

"I brought you a present."

I wrinkled my nose a bit, "What?"

He pulled out one of the files and slid it across the table, "Why don't you open it and see."

I opened the file and there was a leather binder inside, I opened it. Inside the binder was my Bachelor's degree in Business Administration from Valparaiso, it was dated June 1970. I looked at it in shock, "How...?"

"Sandra, we're the FBI. Don't underestimate us." He smiled. "It comes with a positive employment reference from the FBI from July 1970 until after you testify, your reason for leaving us will be to pursue other interests." He pulled his lip up and stuck out his two front teeth and put his hands up on either side of his face, his fingers curled like claws. "How are the rats doing now?" He wrinkled his nose.

I laughed. "Much better; now what?" I asked as I ran my hand over my diploma.

"Sandra, what I was trying to tell you was if anything else happens, if you kill anyone else, our deal under witness protection is out. Understand?"

"Yes, but I'm not sure about California now that Robert Allen's gone."

"We've got some time between now and when the trials begin, you have to decide what you want to do and where you want to be."

"How much time?"

"Six to twelve months or maybe longer, unless there's some sort of deal cut."

"Deal? What the hell are you talking about?"

"It's always a possibility Sandra, you know that, but in this case I doubt it. The syndicate was so large, the girls so young, our perps so highly placed and our evidence so strong that I'd bet the bureau pushes hard on this. Have you seen the papers? Eric pushed another file over in front of me. It had articles about the busts from newspapers in Florida, South Carolina, North Carolina, and Tennessee.

"Coffee?" Emma asked as the door opened and she brought in a tray with a coffee pot, mugs, cream, and sugar.

I looked up. Emma was such a class woman, "Emma, I'm sorry about the phone call the last time we spoke, you have always been..."

"Oh honey," she started in her deep, eloquent southern voice, "after what you've been through, there's no need to apologize to me." She put the tray down on the table in front of me and opened up her arms.

I stood up and we hugged. "You've been a good daughter these past two years."

I don't know whether it was the reference to our phone relationship, her remark, the stress of the last few days or just being hugged, but I started to cry. Eric looked shocked. Emma rubbed my back and told me that everything was going to be all right, but I just lost it. I started blurting out what had happened with Tony and my mom. Emma and I sat down and after a few minutes of my blubbering and explaining what happened with Tony, she handed me a napkin to blow my nose while Eric sat on the opposite side of the table and stayed out of the way by pretending to be reading the files.

I finished with, "What if I lose him Emma, Oh God I couldn't take that."

"Sandra, honey, now listen to me. You can never lose your family as long as there is love. You love your son and he loves you. He's thirteen and he's just been shocked by the truth. He'll need some time and distance before he can deal with it and you're not finished here yet, are you?"

Eric looked up, "Not yet, maybe as long as another year."

"You're thirty-two years old, Sandra. You still have a whole lifetime ahead of you. Just hang in there a bit longer, then, you can start your new life. Think you can do that?"

"Yes."

"Good." She smiled and rubbed my upper arm, then she offered this, "Be strong, Sandra."

I damn near fell off the chair. What was it with older women and this strength thing!

"Thanks, mom." I managed.

"Emma left and Eric asked, "So where do you want to be? Do you want to go to California now?"

"I just don't know. I guess I need some time to sort things out. I need to start to figure out my personal life. Give me a few days to get the lay of the land so to speak."

"I don't like you not being in the program now, Sandra. You're a witness and some of these guys will make bail. You have to be very careful."

"I will. Just a few days, Eric."

"Where are you staying?"

"I'm at Billy Arrowood's cabin."

"Take to the end of the week. I'll see you here next Monday morning."

"That will be fine." I picked up my diploma and started towards the door.

Eric turned, "If anything happens, I want..."

"...you to call me right away!" I continued in a deep authoritative voice.

Eric shook his head, "You're killing me, Sandra."

"That would make four." I said as I closed the door.

Billy and I drove back to his cabin. I told him what had happened and he encouraged me to make my peace with Tony. When we got back, there were more than a dozen different rifles, shotguns, and pistols on his porch.

There was a note that read:

Sandra,

In heaven or in hell, I will wait for you.

With all my love,

Robert Allen

It was in his handwriting. I smiled as I pictured Jerry Crosby Miller putting the guns on the porch while we were in Knoxville. I took a 16 gauge double barrel shotgun and Robert Allen's "cherry" M1911 colt .45. The rest I gave to Billy along with the related ammo. Later that night I called my mom in Chicago. During the conversation my mom said, "Sandra, I've tried to explain to him what you did and why. I think he's okay with the FBI and your helping young girls, it's the prostitution and lying to him that has him so upset. It's a trust broken Sandra, he's hurt and angry."

"What did he say? Can I talk to him?"

"Sandra, he needs time, he needs..."

"Mother, please put him on the line, let me talk to him, please."

"Sandra, he doesn't want to talk to you now."

"Mother, I want to talk to Tony. I want to talk to my son, now. Where is he?"

I heard my mother's voice through the phone, "Tony, please...come talk to your mother."

I could hear my son's response as he shouted at his grandmother, "NO...I TOLD YOU I DON'T WANT TO TALK TO HER ANYMORE! I DON'T WANT TO SEE HER! STOP ASKING ME!"

The words hurt, the pain was worse than anything I had ever felt. "Okay mother...okay...please...stop... please...please...s-stop..." I broke down and I felt someone take the phone from my hand. I looked up; it was Billy.

"Sandra will call back again." He said in his inimitable way. Then he hung up. I cried. I felt like I was losing my mind.

We spent the next five hours talking about our families and we spent the next few days walking in the woods.

I think that the peace and serenity of the woods was a stark contrast to the last two years of my life. I asked Billy to teach me everything he knew about the wilderness. He told me that it would take years to teach everything because in order to learn, you must experience the outdoors. This thought stayed in my mind the rest of the week.

On Monday, I met with Eric again. I told him I had made my decision. I told him about what I was going

through with Tony and that Billy had offered to let me
stay with him. Eric didn't like the idea, but he offered
no resistance. We arranged to keep in touch and for
the money Mrs. Lewis had been receiving to be put in
an account for me in Knoxville along with the forty-five
hundred I still had from Santee. I called my mother to
let her know that she would continue to receive the
other two hundred dollars a week for Tony. I told her
she could contact me through the FBI office in
Knoxville, but that I would not be calling for a while.

She understood.

My Year In The Mountains

Billy and I did some shopping in Knoxville at an outfitter's store. He picked and I paid. We bought some waterproof hiking boots, another backpack with a lightweight pot and utensils, a sleeping bag, a Swiss Army knife, a Buck knife, an E-Tool, camouflage undershirt and pants and a hat. We bought several cans of food with Sterno cans, a waterproof container for matches, a canteen, and a compass. We picked up ammo for my guns and a few other items. He told me that he wanted me to learn how to survive in the woods. Surprising to me, everything we purchased didn't weigh much more than my shotgun and Billy taught me how to pack and carry so my load was balanced even when I was wearing my parka. This is critical if you are hiking in the wilderness.

When we got back, he gave me fishing hooks in a plastic bag along with weights and some monofilament fishing line. Billy also put a strap on the shotgun for me. We spent three overnights in the woods. Billy taught me how to use the compass, when to fish and hunt and what was much more important, he taught me how to track. I think he enjoyed having someone to share his knowledge with; it must have been similar to how Indians taught each new generation. Of all the things I learned from Billy, the most important thing was how to move in the woods, quietly.

We sat in front of a fire and talked. Billy held Jerry Crosby Miller. "Sandra, the animals see better, hear better and smell better than we do. They run, fly, or swim faster than we can. This is their home; we are just visitors. We must use our brain and our stealth to succeed. If you do not use these gifts, you will die in the wilderness. Do you understand?"

"Yes, but there is so much to learn."

"You learn well, Sandra, you are a survivor. You have the heart of a warrior. I am proud to be your friend."

"Thank you, Billy, and I am proud to have a friend like you."

Each day and night I learned something different, which I added to the knowledge I had from my previous hikes with him. There is something about my experience in the forest that I can't, to this day, explain, but the forest brought me peace. There, I never drank or felt the need to drink.

On July 28, 1972, Judge John McGranahan made bail. His brother and two nephews were also out and looking for me. I was oblivious to what was happening, as I had not left Billy's cabin or the woods in almost two weeks. My face had healed and whether it was the outdoors or my not wearing any makeup, I felt I still looked pretty. Billy said it was living without the stress I had been under during the last two years.

On Thursday August 3, Billy, Jerry Crosby Miller, and me were returning to the cabin around 8pm. We had been on a two-day hike. We approached the cabin from the ridge behind it and then dropped down onto a bench just above the cabin. Suddenly, Billy stopped. He turned and put his finger to his lips, then he slowly lowered himself into a squatting position, I followed suit behind him and slightly to his left. I picked Jerry up and looked down at the cabin, but couldn't see anything wrong.

My Year In The Mountains

We stayed absolutely still for about ten minutes before
I saw a man move from behind a tree next to the
cabin. I just about shit myself. How had Billy seen
him? I had this urge to slip behind a red oak tree
about three feet off to our left so I wouldn't be seen,
but Billy had taught me while we hunted, "The first
one to move loses." Every feeling that I had from that
night in Freddy's trailer came rushing back to me. I
could hear my heart beating out of my mouth. I looked
at Billy, frozen like a rock, as he stared at the cabin
over two hundred yards away. I tried to mimic him.
Then I saw movement to the right of the cabin.
Another man was standing behind a tree taking a leak.

A few minutes later, the first man waved his hand and
suddenly, three other men stepped out from hiding
places around the cabin. They all gathered in the
fading light, talked for a minute or so, and then left
following the path to the main road. I learned the
value of stealth that day; it saved my life!

The men had been inside the cabin, but there was
nothing there of mine. Everything I owned either was
in my car or on my back as Billy had insisted I carry
my stuff on our hikes so I could get use to the weight.
Billy and I stayed up late that night talking. I told him I
would leave in the morning. He didn't like the idea, but
he understood. We knew the men would come back.
He told me he would contact Eric Marsh and that if I
was needed, he'd come and find me.

In the morning, Billy fixed me breakfast. I got my
things and stepped out onto the porch. Billy was
sitting on his rocker whittling a piece of wood.

"We're leaving now, Billy."

He never looked up, "Yup." He kept on whittling.

I turned and left. Halfway up the hill Jerry Crosby Miller started meowing. His meows echoed down the hill on the warm summer morning.

The first few days in the forest were exciting. Being on my own, caring for Jerry and myself, was an adventure. We hiked over towards Bear Cave Hollow. The first day I simply hiked. For dinner, Jerry and I had a can of beans I had in my pack, but I went to sleep hungry. The next morning I was up early and went hunting. Jerry and I split a squirrel for breakfast. We hiked all day, moving slowly and quietly through the woods. We had to cross two roads on the way and we waited until there were no cars in sight before we crossed. I tried my hand at fishing and caught two rainbow trout that I cleaned and cooked over a fire. Nevertheless, at night, when I was all alone with my thoughts, I cried. I cried a lot. Sometimes I thought about killing myself. I would be with Robert Allen then. Had I made the right decisions, where was my life going? I had dreams, horrible dreams of Norman and bad things I don't wish to share. I remember swearing that I would do something good with the rest of my life if I were given a second chance.

I would wake up the next morning to the beauty of the forest and the purring of Jerry Crosby Miller. It has always been fascinating to me how our pets love us, unconditionally. "A new day, thank you, Lord. I'll take it." I thought.

We walked another day. It was summer and occasionally we would hear other hikers in the woods-we heard them, they never saw us. Late in the afternoon, Jerry started acting crazy. He ran off to the side of me and up a tree. He sat on a branch no higher than I was and began a low, rumbling meow. I looked around and realized we had come up on the backside of Bear Cave Hollow. Jerry had not forgotten our previous experience with the old black bear.

We set up camp across the stream from the cave. It brought back memories of Tony's visit the year before. As I was setting up camp and gathering wood, Jerry disappeared. I was worried about him and went looking for him immediately. He was nowhere to be found. Then I heard him meowing. It was coming from the cave. It only took me a minute to decide what to do. I grabbed my shotgun and flashlight and splashed across the creek like the cavalry. By then, it was getting toward night and there wasn't much light filtering into the entrance. I called out for Jerry and I heard him meow. I flashed the light up ahead of me with both barrels ready to go; I could smell bear and feces as I slowly walked back into the cave. The cave had two sections; the second section was smaller than the first. When I got to the second part I saw Jerry...lying on top of the bear! The stench was horrible; the bear was dead.

I picked up Jerry and headed back to camp. The next morning I thought, "If I can get the bear out and get the cave cleaned up a bit what a great hideout it would make!"

Old Mr. Bear was over three hundred pounds. I had a deer drag rope, but he was too heavy for me to drag, so I lightened the load. I used my E-Tool to cut him into two manageable size pieces and then dragged them out. I skinned two pieces of fur off with my Buck knife and after wetting them in the creek and spreading them in the sun for a few days, Jerry and I had two nice mattresses to sleep on. I used the E-Tool to dig a hole and bury him. The next few days I concentrated on cleaning the cave. When it was ready, I moved from my lean-to across the stream to the front part of the cave where I set up a fire ring and burned some herbs I found from where Tony and I saw Branch Earl the year before. The cave actually smelled good.

Slowly, I was building my confidence. As summer turned to fall, the grandeur of the fall foliage became breathtaking. Each day the new red, yellow, and orange leaves presented themselves in a cornucopia of color; the display was simply awesome and my heart filled with joy as I marveled at God's creation. Then fall turned to winter and my hunting skills became better and better. Billy had been right, the more I experienced the forest, the better my skills became.

At night, I would think about my life and try to concentrate on the positives. I had a wonderful son, a loving mother, and I made friends easily. I was in good health for someone thirty-two years old. I had a good education and I had an excellent work ethic. I felt I was missing two things, someone to love, and someone to love me. I wanted someone to take care of and someone who would take care of me. It always brought me back to Robert Allen; I missed him so.

As the seasons change in the mountains, so does survival. The cave was great shelter and fishing was always good, I just needed to dig deeper for worms. In the winter the forest changes, it is easier for the hunter. Leaves are down and vision is greater, animals are easier to track and see in snow and you can move quietly much faster. You can also still hunt, up in a tree or behind a log just off a trail. Tracks, rubbings and poop, that's what you look for, and when you find it, you sit and wait. I was a little down at Christmas, not being able to see Tony and my mom, but I was starting to get used to being alone. I bagged a turkey on Christmas Eve morning and Jerry and I ate turkey, acorns, and Jerusalem artichokes for two days. I kept my spirit up by thinking about something Billy had said on one of our hiking trips, "I never met anyone whose future was behind them." As the New Year began, I felt myself getting strong; I had no fear.

By spring, I had adapted to living in the mountains. I became acquainted with a number of poor mountain families. It was not unusual to find ten or twelve people living in a two-room cabin with no running water and no electricity. The men and women looked old beyond their years. Some of the families had a potbelly stove and some of them only had a fireplace for heating and cooking.

I met Ray Carpenter while I was hunting. It was late February and I had just taken a six-point buck. I was field dressing the deer when I heard a noise behind me. I turned and saw a cougar. I reached for my gun as he charged at me, but before I reached it, a shot rang out. The cat dropped about twenty feet from me. I turned to see where the shot came from and there stood this tall skinny old man with a full gray beard, a dirty old Woolrich coat, and a baseball hat.

"T-thanks," I stammered.

"Welcome," he said then spit a tobacco chew in the snow. "He'd been stalking you, girl."

I reached over to pick up my gun and his gun swung up towards me. I picked up my gun and stood up, "That's a fine shotgun you got there. You don't see those old single shot guns around anymore."

He lowered his gun and smiled, "You know your guns don't you girl."

"I...well...listen, I won't need all this meat. Give me a hand and I'll take a quarter and you can have the rest."

"You listen here now, I don't take any charity. That's your kill."

"Charity! How do I repay you for saving my life?"

He stood there for a while rubbing his beard, then he said, "You gotta deal, girl."

Ray lived in a small cabin with his wife and six children. One of his girls had two children that lived there. She had no husband, and I never inquired. I spent some time with the Carpenters that spring. They taught me about planting and cultivating a garden. It was nice being part of a family. I liked it...a lot.

In all the years I lived in Tennessee, I never once saw or heard of any social worker or doctor that visited these people and tried to help them. There were welfare agencies, but the families that lived thirty-five or forty miles from the nearest town had no transportation to get there. As far as getting any aid to them, it was as if they didn't exist. I know this to be true because of my contact with these families.

The mountain people weren't lazy. They were just poor. They hunted, planted a garden and to get cash, some made moonshine. The making of bootleg whiskey comes under the jurisdiction of the Alcohol, Tobacco, and Firearms Division of the Justice Department. At that time, the first offense meant a year in jail, the second offense five years, the third offense ten years. If the guilty party was convicted a fourth time, he got life; life for making liquor. The penalty was because the government wasn't getting its tax money. I found it curious that they didn't go into the mountains to help poor people, but they could go into the mountains to arrest them.

In late July of 1973, I decided to go see Billy and find out what was going on with the trial. Before I left I dropped by the Carpenter's home and gave Ray's wife a hundred dollars. I told her it was for her hospitality and for Ray saving me from the cougar. She told me that she could now buy new shoes for all the children. It made me feel great; giving is so much better than receiving. I saw Ray on the way out. He asked me, "Were you Robert Allen's girl, Sandra?"

"Yes, Ray, I was his woman. You knew Robert Allen?"

"My nephew was a good man. He helped us out here two winters ago, after Christmas. You did good when you killed those men." Ray spit his chew.

"Nephew?"

"Rebecca's my little sis." Ray spit again.

"Mystery unveiled," I thought. I found out where Robert Allen had been for a month. We shook hands, "You take good care now," I said.

I hiked all day and Jerry and I camped out overnight. I no longer had any fear of the forest; I felt it was my second home. The next day I reached Billy's. I remember coming down the ridge behind the cabin. I could see him on the front porch in his rocker. I crept quietly down the hill and as I came up on the cabin, I let Jerry Crosby Miller down and he started to creep towards the porch. Before he got there, Billy said, "You are a very special cat, Jerry Crosby Miller. There are few who could sneak up on an Indian."

"How do you do that; how did you know I was coming?" I stepped up on the porch and hugged my friend.

"You really want to know, don't you?"

"Please."

"Old Indian secret; sit in my chair and I will tell you."

I sat in his chair and he stepped off the porch and began to walk up the hill. He got about twenty yards up the hill before he shouted, "Look at my truck."

Billy had his truck parked in front of the cabin. The passenger side window was up. If you looked at it, you could see the reflection of anything coming down the hill behind the cabin.

"Cheater, cheater pumpkin eater," I laughed as he walked back.

"Come inside, there is much to talk about."

Billy told me that the men had returned two times. He told them he had not seen me and that he thought I had returned to Chicago. They had tried to catch him by surprise, but he had gotten the drop on them each time. The last time he told them if they came back, he would shoot them; they did not return.

Eric Marsh and Joe Holt had visited Billy, too. The trial was to start Monday, September 11, and they wanted to prepare my testimony. The next day was Thursday, July 27. I had Billy drop me off at the FBI Office in Knoxville in the morning. I walked in not having had a bath, except for the streams in the forest, in over a year. Emma looked up, "Can I help you."

"Hello, Mom, it's me, Sandra."

Emma's mouth dropped wide open as she gasped, "Oh my God, Sandra?"

She really did not want to hug me, but she stood up and said, "Thank God you're alright. Stay there, I'll get Eric now." She called back to Eric's office, "Eric, Sandra Love is here to see you." In less than a minute, five men came out of the back office door, Eric and Joe, the Agent in Charge, and two attorneys.

"I don't even want to ask, do I?" Eric stood there scratching his head and staring at me. I had on my camouflage undershirt and hat, my really bad jeans, my dirty hiking boots, and my belt with my buck knife still on it. If I had wanted to make an impression, I had.

One of the attorneys, an older man, asked, "Is any of that human blood?"

"No, just bear, deer, and mine." I pointed at some blood on my thigh and winked at Joe. The attorneys just stared; Joe and Eric smiled. "So who do I have to kill in order to get a drink and a cigarette around here?" I put my hand on the hilt of my Buck knife.

The Agent in Charge introduced himself and the two attorneys. "It is a pleasure to meet you, Sandra. I'm Todd Brennaman and these two gentlemen are Ken Mosley and Bob Griffith from the Attorney General's Office. I would be pleased to get you both a drink and a cigarette. Eric, will you and Joe see Sandra into the conference room?" As Eric, Joe, and I went into the conference room, Joe Holt turned to me and whispered, "Nice outfit, Armani?"

We sat in the conference room for a few minutes. Eric told me my mother had called twice, once at

Christmas and again about a month ago. I thanked him for the information. He asked me if I wanted to call her. I told him I had the number.

The other three joined us and the Agent in Charge had a tumbler with ice and vodka in it and a pack of Marlboros and a lighter. "Vodka, am I correct?"

"Yes, thank you." I sipped the vodka slowly- it had been a year. The first cigarette gave me a buzz. At first, we talked about the last year. I shared some general information about where I was and how I had been living. Then we got down to business.

The most important thing they wanted was that both Freddy's testimony and mine agreed; there could be no conflicts. They set up a schedule of meetings in a safe house they had just outside Knoxville. Freddy was already living there with four agents on duty twenty four-seven. Before I went there, I told them that I'd have to fix up a bit. I gave them the spare key I kept for my Firebird so that they could get my luggage, then Agent Eric Marsh and Agent Joseph Holt took me to a salon in Knoxville and waited while I got a facial, my hair washed and trimmed, a manicure and a pedicure, and a massage. I felt like the Queen of Sheba. However, when I was done, I still had to put my hunting clothes back on. When I got to the safe house, my luggage was there. I went to my room and hung up all my clothes and then I went into the bathroom. I showered for an hour; it was glorious.

I dressed and put on some makeup and looked in the mirror, it was me- the new me! I went down stairs and out into the dining room. Two agents were eating dinner with Freddy.

"Oh my, God, I thought you were dead." He stood up and started towards me, one of the agents stepped in between us.

"It's okay," I said. Freddy looked drawn. We hugged each other.

"Please sit here, Sandra," he asked as he pulled out the chair next to him. I sat down. "You look great, where have you been?"

I laughed for five minutes.

******

As it turned out, John McGranahan and his brother received life sentences. Fourteen other men including pimps from Florida, South Carolina, and Tennessee received sentences ranging from ten to forty years. The press had a field day and the feds had their Heyday. Freddy and I had our day in court, too, but the most surprising part was the number of underage girls that testified. I sat in court and watched as they told their stories, some cried, some were matter of fact, all were relieved when they returned to a free life.

When it was all over, I told Eric that I would take a pass on the witness protection program. California had been a dream I shared with Robert Allen, without him I wouldn't go. No one knew my son or mother's name nor did they have a chance of finding them, so long as I stayed away. A green-eyed woman with reddish blonde hair and a black cat stand out in a crowd. I didn't worry about them as long as I stayed away from Chicago. Eric was true to his word and arranged a job for me in Charlotte, North Carolina.

A couple of days after the trial, I asked Billy to pick me up at the FBI office. He brought my cat, Jerry Crosby

Miller along, too. I left with another eight hundred dollars I received when the feds arranged for the disposition of my car. I closed my bank account and had a little over thirty-five thousand, a suitcase full of clothes, two pistols, a shotgun, and my degree to show for my adventure in Newport. Billy drove me to Charlotte; I was ready to begin my new life.

A New Life

I was thirty-three years old in the fall of 1973 when I went to work in a bank in Charlotte, North Carolina. I started as a Loan Officer. I moved up to Assistant Branch Manager in 1975 and then to Branch Manager in 1977. I enjoyed the work and helping people with financial problems.

I bought a black 1971 Ford Torino with nine thousand miles on it. I rented an apartment in a new apartment complex outside the city and shopped at malls again. Socially, I dated and made friends with some of the girls who worked at the bank. I began dying my hair a bit darker, auburn brown and I cut it in a shag-cut like Jane Fonda had in the movie Klute. I thought it was a bit more conservative than my natural reddish blonde hair; I couldn't do anything about my big green eyes.

Christmas 1973, I spent in Chicago. It's hard for me to talk about this, so if I don't make much sense please forgive me. I had made my mistakes, but I also had done some good. I needed forgiveness. Tony was a freshman in high school; he was President of his class and an outstanding athlete, particularly in baseball. I think we all remember what it's like to be a teenager; everything is black and white, right and wrong, clear as a bell, there's no compromising. It's not until we get older that things start to gray up a bit, that you learn that win-win is just so much better than win-lose. I was hoping that at Christmas, I could find that win-win.

Tony was fourteen.

I arranged for a cat-sitter, Janet, to take care of Jerry Crosby Miller over the holiday. I flew from Charlotte to

Chicago on Saturday December 22, and got in around 1pm. My mom and Tony greeted me at the airport.

"Sandra!"

"Mom," I answered.

My mom and I hugged while Tony hung back. I looked over at him; his face was neutral.

"Hi."

"Hi," He responded.

"How's Sally Myers doing?"

He started to smile, and then said, "She got fat."

"It happens." I walked over to my son, put my hands on his arms, looked up into his eyes, and said, "A lot of things happen in life that are bad; sometimes you just have to forgive and go on. Please forgive me, Tony, I love you more than anything in the world."

Tony's eyes welled up with tears and he grabbed me and hugged me as he cried, "Mom, why...why?"

I pushed him away and said, "Let's go to lunch and I will answer any question you have about my life."

Tony smiled as he wiped his eyes, "How's McDonald's?" He asked.

"Whatever you like."

The three of us locked arms; my mother was on one side of me, and my son on the other as we walked toward baggage. My mother was 5'7", Tony was now 5'8 and I was in the middle at 5'3", but I felt seven feet tall. We must have been a sight; I was walking on my yellow brick road. We didn't talk much while we walked. I thought about last year's Christmas in the wilderness and squeezed both their arms tight, and then the memory faded.

We had lunch at McDonald's; it had been a long time since I had a cheeseburger and fries that tasted that good. Tony and I talked about everything from my rape at fifteen to working for The Outfit and then the job in Newport. I told him about where I had been living for the last year. Lord, I will never forget the looks on their faces as I told them about my adventure. I am sure our two-hour lunch was the longest in fast-food history.

I had brought a folder full of newspaper clippings on the bust and the trial for them to read. Tony glanced at them and then said, "I don't care what you did, I love you, mom."

I have never had a better Christmas present.

We shopped and went home; the visit went well. I explained to Tony and my mother that after the trial my choices were to enter the witness protection program and take them with me away from Chicago or live on my own and be careful about visiting Chicago or any type of publicity. I think they understood. After that, I talked to my family every Sunday night, and we were always together for vacations and holidays. As Tony matured and became an adult, he gained a better perspective on my life.

In March 1976, I met my second husband, Gunnery Sergeant Michael L Horne. Michael was stationed at Camp Lejuene in Jacksonville, North Carolina, and was visiting his parents in Charlotte on St. Patrick's

Day. We met in a bar downtown and started dating.
Michael was 5'6" and weighed about 165 pounds, he
was built like so many Marines with a hard muscular
build and that squared off jaw and chiseled
features...he reminded me of Billy. I liked rubbing his
head; his short hair felt funny and it made me giggle.
Oh, and he loved Jerry Crosby Miller. They got along
as if they had been friends for life.

Michael was fine with the bed business, too; he had a
lot of stamina, although from time to time he'd ask,
"Where did you learn to do that?" I'd just distract him
with a ball game or some news item; I don't think I
ever told him a lot about my past.

We dated for over a year. He met Tony and my mom
in the summer of 1977 while they were visiting. Tony
and Mom seemed to like him and they enjoyed
Michael's stories about when he had deployed.
Michael and I were the same age, but he looked
younger than I did. By the way, don't you hate how
men think they look more distinguished as they age,
but women just get old? What's with that?

Anyway, we saw each other every other weekend
mostly in Charlotte because he could also see his
folks while he was home, but in the summer, I would
visit him because he lived near the beach. The North
Carolina coast south of the Outer Banks to below
Jacksonville is known as the Crystal Coast. It is
absolutely one of the prettiest places I had ever seen.
The water and beaches are clear, warm, and beautiful.

Michael asked me to marry him and I said yes. I liked
Michael a lot; he was handsome, sexy, fun to be with,
and offered me something that I only ever felt with
Robert Allen. He offered to take care of me. We were
married in the fall of 1977. I left my job and we moved

to the little town of Peletier where we bought some ground that bordered on the Croatan National Forest and put a brand new trailer on it.

Did you say happy? The forest, the beach, I didn't have to work and I was a Marine Corp wife- cool beans! It meant I had access to shopping on the base at Camp Lejeune as well as health and dental care. My life was good and the gravy on the potatoes was that Tony had received a four-year academic scholarship to Illinois University. Their business school boasts Presidents and CEOs of McDonald's, General Motors, United Airlines, and Disney Studios.

Then in March of 1978, Michael deployed with his MEU. I stood on the tarmac with hundreds of other Marine Corp wives, some with children and some without, all of whom kissed their husbands good-bye and watched as they flew off. Amid the tears, I stood there; I was so proud of my husband. He would be gone for eight or nine months. I really had not made too many friends with other Marine Corp wives; there was a huge difference between living on base and living off base, and frankly, it was a bit cliquish.

Once again, I found myself alone in the woods. I enjoyed hiking and when the weather got warm, I went to the beach. I was enjoying my life. I took a volunteer job at the Carteret County animal shelter. I loved working with the animals and found many of my friends and neighbors willing to adopt rather than see an animal euthanized.

Then in the fall of 1978, I got a call from my mom. She had been diagnosed with liver cancer and needed care. I sent a letter to Michael explaining what was happening and made the appropriate calls to the base, for change of contact information. Then I flew up to

Chicago the first week of October; Jerry Crosby Miller came with me.

Although my mom and Tony had visited me for their July vacation that year, the woman who answered the door at my mother's house did not look anything like the woman who had been in my home for a month that summer.

"Mom!" I hugged her. She was pale, almost yellow, and drawn.

"Sandra." My mother looked at my astonished face...and wept. I held her and then she looked at my luggage and my cat cage, "Come in, come in. I'm so glad you're here."

She had a bed set up in the living room where she could watch TV. I sat beside the bed and held her hand, "I'm here for you, mom," I told her and then we talked. She told me that the one thing she had worried about was dying alone. I told her, "That will never happen while I breathe." The doctors told my mom that she only had a few weeks left.

Just in case there are people reading my story who have lost a loved one to cancer, I won't relive the nightmare of seeing my mother die from the disease. For those of you, who haven't lived through it, pray to God that you never have to experience it. As you know from what I've told you, I have had my share of death in my life, all of which was sudden violent death. This was something entirely different and much more painful.

In November, my mom had a hospice nurse visiting everyday to check on her pain medications. She was on a morphine drip that she could use herself by pushing a button on the line. Slowly, she was moving in and out of consciousness; when she was awake, I sat and held her hand and prayed for her. Tony came back from college on weekends to be with us. On November 22, I received a phone call from Michael. He was injured in a field exercise and had broken his right leg and hip. The Corps was flying him home and he wanted me to be there to take care of him. I explained the situation with my mom and told him I just could not be there for him. He was upset; I don't think he ever forgave me.

My mom died on Christmas Eve at 11am, with Tony, myself, and the hospice nurse present. It was the worst Christmas of my life.

I spent the next two weeks attending to the funeral arrangements and the estate issues. Against my son's concerns, I attended the funeral. I saw my father for the first time in almost thirty years. We spoke briefly and I introduced him to his grandson.

I went home and cared for Michael. He never fully recovered from his injury and by the end of 1979, he received a full disability discharge from the Marine Corps. During that time, Michael began drinking regularly. I tried to help him, but we became more distant every day. I was not drinking. In January of 1980, Michael moved to Charlotte and filed for divorce. I was very sad; I thought I must be a bad wife and a bad woman. I never asked him for a dime of his pension. He had earned every cent of it. In return, he gave me his share of the property we lived on. During the year, I received twenty thousand dollars from my mother's estate. I put it in the bank and never told Michael.

Tony was between his junior and senior year when he came to visit me late that summer. He had been working for an investment firm doing his required internship. He told me that he enjoyed it very much. He also told me that he had met a girl that he was serious about. I was very proud of him. He was only able to stay two weeks before his fall classes began. He noticed my sadness and urged me to sell my property and move back north, but I didn't want to move back to Chicago as it brought back bad memories. I loved the Crystal Coast and the Croatan National Forest, so I began to adopt animals from the shelter. I started building a new family, my family.

My first two dogs were Zack and Cooper, two Walker Hounds. Walker Hounds is short for Treeing Walker Coonhounds, great hunting dogs. I took Jerry Crosby Miller to the shelter with me to help pick them out. They were a pair and I took them in the forest with me every day. At night, I had them in the trailer. They were only six months old and they needed some love; so did I.

In May of 1981, I attended Tony's graduation. He introduced me to Julie and the next year I took my last trip up to Chicago for their wedding. I guess it would be fair to say that Tony and I live in two very different worlds. He has become very successful and I am proud of him. He has often asked me to come back to Chicago, but I am dug in "like a tick" and will probably die here.

My life has gone downhill these past five years. I have held many types of jobs and I've gone back to drinking. I suffer from depression and when I drink, I usually get in trouble. I get lonely and when I do, I'll take a man; I sure as hell don't get a hundred dollars from them anymore. I remember one night at The

Court, a customer accidently let Jerry Crosby Miller out of my room. I refused to work until I found my cat. I had three men looking everywhere for him before they found him up in a tree. This middle age burley truck driver climbed up in the tree, out on a limb, and brought him down. What men will do for sex! Politically, I've noticed whenever there is a scandal in Washington, if it's about sex, it's the left wing guys, if it's about money it's the right wing guys. I've learned a lot about human behavior, especially the nature of men. They are driven by three things sex, sex, and sex, but who am I to criticize God's design?

Speaking of God, I do attend services when I'm sober enough to do so. I always thought it inconvenient that Sunday morning came so quickly after Saturday night. I've been attending church at Spring Garden Missionary Baptist Church on Bogue Loop Road for the past year. All the members, with the exception of me and another woman are black. I've been made to feel welcome even after all that crap in the newspapers about Michael Shornock and me.

When my husband Michael and I first lived here, I attended at the all-white Missionary Baptist Church near where we lived. There are certainly differences between the two congregations. Folks at Spring Garden Missionary Baptist Church dress up more for church services. Black women wear their Sunday best including hats and gloves and black men are always in a suit and tie. In the all-white Missionary Baptist Church, Sunday dress is a bit more informal. Women do not wear hats or gloves and men wear slacks and dress shirts; very rarely did I see a tie or jacket...I don't think the Lord cares.

I just seem to enjoy the service at Spring Garden Missionary Baptist Church more; it's livelier with a lot of joyous noise and a lot less fire and brimstone. I like the singing, swaying, and clapping; it makes me happy for a while. I do not think church once a week will make the difference between heaven and hell, so I talk to God every day. I try to avoid asking him for stuff. Instead, when I'm alone in the forest, I thank him for all I have been given.

In 1984, my cat, Jerry Crosby Miller, died of old age. He was fourteen. Although I like the cats I have now, none of them has ever been as close to me as Jerry. I miss him, but have no regrets. I treated him well.

There is no retirement plan for 'ladies of the evening.' In spite of all the money I made, in the end most of us have nothing. As age creeps up and finally catches up with us, we have few marketable skills with which to support ourselves. It's a dead-end job and a dead-end life.

I feel I have been luckier than most. I have friends who help me and I have my animals who I love and in return they love me and accept me as I am. I don't know that a person can really expect more out of life than that.

Kat, this is important. I want you to know that even though I took a lot of wrong turns and did a lot of bad things, I consider my life's work to be Tony, not prostitution. And I am very proud of my life's work."

 The room was silent. I looked over at the tape recorder; it was on and the tape was turning, Sandra had finished her story. I looked at what I had just typed; the tears came quickly.

The Truth

I needed to make a decision. Sandra's story was fantastic. It was everything you would want in either a novel or a movie; part Greek tragedy, part pulp fiction. A strong female character, dramatic storyline sprinkled with humor, sex and violence galore, redeeming social values, and it was all based on a true story...or was it? How much of this story was true and how much of it was conceived in that brilliant, yet alcohol impaired mind. I really did not know whether I had come across something very special or the grandiose delusions of a manic-depressive personality.

Then there was the other issue. I had been seeing Sandra for almost six months. When she was sober, she was the sweetest, kindest, and smartest woman I knew. We had become friends. When she was drunk, she was the most outlandish, manipulative, and potentially violent character I had ever met. She was two entirely different women in one body.

Hank and I had dinner out that evening.

"This is a really great story, but I can't present it as a biography, it's got to be a novel."

"Why?" Hank responded as he turned from looking out the window as the sun set on Bogue Sound.

"Because I don't know whether any of this is true. I'm going to meet with Sandra tomorrow and give her the final chapter, but then we're going to have to have this out."

"Christ, Kat, don't get confrontational with Sandra, you know her reputation."

"I don't want any confrontation; she would probably just tell me to go over to..." Suddenly, the light came on. Lord, it is a glorious thing when you have a great idea! "I wonder if she'd be willing to go back to Newport with me."

"Oh Kat, come on, don't you think that might be a bit on the dangerous side?"

"Hank, it's been thirteen years; do you think anyone cares anymore?"

"Don't know, but I know you, Kat, you're going to find out with or without Sandra aren't you?"

I held out my drink and said, "Honey, you are the most perceptive man on this planet. Cheers!"

******

I went to my Editor at the paper and asked for a week off. He hemmed and hawed, and then told me to go. It was late April of 1987, when I took the last chapter over to Sandra.

"Kat, this is great. I don't seem too whiney, do I?" Sandra asked as we sat out on the two tree stumps.

"Honey, after that story I'd think it impossible for anyone to think you're whiney."

"Good. What's the next step?" Sandra asked, her face lit up like a child's.

"If you needed to go away for awhile, who would take care of your animals?"

Those big green eyes narrowed fast, "Where would I be going, Kat?"

"This is just a first draft Sandra. It's very biographical. I may have to change some things in it in order to get it published. It would then become a novel based on a true story."

"Kat, where would I be going?"

God, that woman had a way of cutting through bullshit.

"If I have to change anything in a second or third draft, I'd like to see the area you've been talking about."

"You want me to go back to Newport with you?"

"Yes."

Sandra jumped up, "I can get my friends to take care of the animals. I'll be ready to go in an hour!" I had never seen Sandra that excited before.

"How's tomorrow sound?"

"Oh, God, Kat, we're going to have an adventure!" She hugged me.

The next day Sandra and I traveled to Newport and stayed overnight. The next day she showed me around town, including The Court, and took me up to The Smokey Mountain Club. The rock walls were still there, but it had never been rebuilt. We drove over to Billy Arrowood's cabin, but he was not there. We went inside and looked around; she said he still lived there. Sandra asked me for a pen and paper, then, she wrote him a short note and left it on the table in the kitchen. Everything was as she described it.

We spent another day visiting Robert Allen's parents' home. Rebecca was there, but Melvin had passed away. The three of us went to the graveyard where Robert Allen was buried, his father beside him. Sandra asked us if she could be alone for a while, so we left her at Robert Allen's grave and waited in the car for about a half an hour. Then she returned and we took Rebecca back home. We spent some time driving around in the mountains. Sandra was quiet for a bit, but then she seemed to snap out of her funk. She took me over to Del Rio and showed me the barn and the cock-fighting ring; everything was as she had described it.

"Can we go to Knoxville, tomorrow? I'd like to see if Eric Marsh is still with the FBI?" Sandra asked.

"Yes, that would be something, wouldn't it?"

The next morning we had breakfast and then drove over to Knoxville. We walked into the FBI office around 10:30 am. A young woman was at the reception desk.

"Is Agent Eric Marsh in today?" Sandra asked.

"I'm sorry; I can't give you that information. May I ask who you are and what is the nature of your business?"

"My name is Sandra Love and I am an old friend in town visiting."

"Like I said, I wouldn't be able to tell you..."

In a flash, Sandra Horne disappeared and Sandra Love came alive. Sandra put both of her hands on the desk, leaned forward into the young woman's face, and growled, "Who's the Agent in Charge now?"

The Truth

"J-Joseph Holt."

"Tell Agent Holt that Sandra Love is here!"

The woman made the call and in less than a minute, Joseph Holt came out to greet us.

"Sandra! Oh my God, how are you? They hugged. "Please come back. It's all right, Carol," he said to the woman at the desk. He turned and looked at me.

"Joe, this is my good friend, Kat. She's writing a novel about our adventure together."

"Well, I'd like to read that when you're through. Come on back."

We went into the conference room. Joe told us that Eric had retired and was now in the Tennessee legislature. Joe even brought out a file with newspaper clippings about the busts, the trial, and Sandra; he made some copies for us. I remember I felt relieved as Sandra and Joe chatted on at length laughing and sharing stories about each other. We stayed about an hour.

On the way home, Sandra asked me to stop at a liquor store. She came out with two pints of vodka. As I drove, Sandra never spoke. She stared out the window at the passing countryside and sipped at the vodka; every once in a while I caught her wiping a tear from her eye.

Sandra and I had become good friends and I tried to help her as best as I could. She lived alone and her life was in decline. She was being treated for clinical depression. There are some stories about Sandra I could tell you, but...well, maybe I will share one or two.

The Outlaw Sandra Love

I remember this one time there was a show in the summer for tourists that was held at an outdoor theater off Peletier Loop Road. It was a reenactment of the birth of Christ called "Worthy is the Lamb". They had all the animals from the Nativity scene including sheep, goats, and even a camel; local actors played the various parts of Mary, Joseph, and the wise men. Sandra helped by taking care of the animals. One evening around 11pm, Joe Willis, the police officer who had been wounded during the bank robbery, was on patrol up Rte 58 when he saw the camel coming down the middle of the road. Riding the camel was The Outlaw Sandra Love.

Epilogue

Sandra and I remained close until the fall of 1992, and then she met Nick. Nick was sixty-five and retired. He owned a boat that he lived on and kept in the town of Swansboro. Sandra and Nick became an item and after a few months, I did not see much of her anymore.

From time to time, they would stop by the house. I live just a block from Bogue Sound, and Hank and I would have dinner with them. Sandra always drank too much. Alcoholism is a disease and an addictive one at that; without help, you are doomed. Sandra never needed help; her motto was, "Be strong."

I have to say that their relationship was cantankerous, but Nick was a good guy and took care of her all the way up until the end.

On Thursday, September 29, 1994, around 2am in the morning, my phone rang. It was Nick; he was in tears.

"Kat, Oh, Kat, she's gone, she's gone...please come over now."

Hank was out of town on business, so I got out of bed and drove the ten minutes up Rte 58 to her lot. I drove onto the dirt road and then down the path to the ridge. An ambulance was there with its flashing red lights illuminating the woods; the lights made the trees look bloody. Two other cars were there, one of them, Nick's.

I went inside and Nick was there. We hugged each other.

The coroner had just arrived.

"Where is my friend?"

Nick, in tears, just pointed to the bedroom.

I went into the bedroom. Sandra lay there on the bed. She was wearing an oversize gray T-shirt that had "USMC" across the front and nothing else. I knelt down beside her. She looked pregnant; she had died of cirrhosis of the liver. When I touched her, she was cold, and I started to cry. Then I felt two hands around my shoulders pull me away. I turned and Nick helped me up and out of the room.

Nick told me that Sandra had not been feeling well that week and that they had been in bed together since early evening kissing and cuddling. Around 1am, Sandra got up to go to the bathroom and on her way back she moaned and collapsed on the bed.

Sandra had made all the arrangements and Nick and I saw after her. Her body was taken to the Jacksonville Hospital and eventually to Fayetteville Community College, Department of Funeral Services Education. Sandra had donated herself to the college to help educate students in the program. Her body was cremated on October 19. Nick and I drove over to Fayetteville on Friday the 21st and received the ashes. On Saturday, Tony and Julie joined us as we stood atop the ridge where her trailer sat and scattered her ashes to the winds, over the forest she loved so much.

******

About The Authors

Kay Roberts Stephens, a native of North Carolina, graduated from East Carolina University with a major in History and a minor in Sociology.

She worked 16 years as a Social Worker; as an avid reader she also became interested in writing. She is the author of a two-volume history of the fishing village of Salter Path which has been purchased by major universities, museums, local residents and tourists visiting in the coastal area of North Carolina.

She is also the author of Raccoon Hill, a novel set in the Northern Piedmont region of North Carolina, based on the lifestyle and events of that era as told to her by her grandmother.

The author, who has been married 44 years, has two grown children and two grandchildren.

Steve Peters was born and raised in suburban Philadelphia. He is a graduate of Penn State University and a Viet Nam veteran. After forty years in Human Resources and Hospital Administration, Steve and his wife, Judy, moved to North Carolina to be close to their grandchildren and North Carolina's beautiful Crystal Coast.

Steve is a member of the Carteret Writers group. He enjoys hunting, fishing, golf and writing. He is the author of many short stories and a children's book, Tyler's Park The Autobiography of a Yellow Lab. This is his first adult fiction novel. Steve and his wife Judy live in Cape Carteret, NC with their two Labrador Retrievers, Zach and Stu.

Contact Steve at slppet@yahoo.com or http://www.TheOutlawSandraLove.com

CPSIA information can be obtained at www.ICGtesting.com
Printed in the USA
BVOW071117100313

315081BV00001B/1/P

9 780615 760315